Olinda Selwyn ... money for her ... ordered luxuries and medicines by the doctor which they cannot afford. As she is an expert embroiderer she answers an advertisement in 'The Times' from a noblewoman who has period beds which need restoration.

Olinda travels to Kelvedon in Derbyshire, one of the most magnificent and treasure-filled houses in England. There she finds that the Dowager Countess is having a love-affair with a man much younger than herself and that her son, the present Earl, has left England because of his disgust at the situation.

How the Earl returns with a French actress and how Olinda becomes involved in a family drama, how she inspires the Earl and helps him through disillusionment and tragedy is told in this 180th book by Barbara Cartland.

OTHER BOOKS BY BARBARA CARTLAND

Romantic Novels, over 290, the most recently published being:

Autobiographical and Biographical:

Historical:

Sociology:

Cookery:
Barbara Cartland's Health Food Cookery Book
Food for Love
Magic of Honey Cookbook
Recipes for Lovers

Editor of:
The Common Problems by Ronald Cartland (with a preface by the
Rt. Hon. the Earl of Selborne, P.C.)
Barbara Cartland's Library of Love
Barbara Cartland's Library of Ancient Wisdom

Drama:
Blood Money
French Dressing

Philosophy:
Touch the Stars

Radio Operetta:
The Rose and the Violet (Music by Mark Lubbock)
performed in 1942

Radio Plays:
The Caged Bird: An episode in the Life of Elizabeth
Empress of Austria. Performed in 1957

General:
Barbara Cartland's Book of Useless Information, with a Foreword
by The Earl Mountbatten of Burma
(in Aid of the United World Colleges)
Love and Lovers (Picture Book)
The Light of Love (Prayer Book)
Barbara Cartland's Scrapbook, in Aid of the Royal Photographic
Museum

Verse:
Lines on Life and Love

Music:
An Album of Love Songs sung with the Royal Philharmonic Orchestra

Magazine:
Barbara Cartland's World of Romance (published in the U.S.A.)

Special Publication:
Love at the Helm
Inspired and helped by Admiral of the Fleet Earl Mountbatten of Burma, in aid of the Mountbatten Memorial Trust

A Dream From the Night

Barbara Cartland

CORGI BOOKS
A DIVISION OF TRANSWORLD PUBLISHERS LTD

A DREAM FROM THE NIGHT

A CORGI BOOK 0 552 10168 0

First publication in Great Britain

PRINTING HISTORY
Corgi edition published 1976
Corgi edition reprinted 1981

Corgi Books are published by
Transworld Publishers Ltd.,
Century House, 61–63 Uxbridge Road,
Ealing, London, W5 5SA
Printed and bound in Great Britain by
Cox & Wyman Ltd, Reading

ABOUT THE AUTHOR

Barbara Cartland, the world's most famous romantic novelist, who is also an historian, playwright, lecturer, political speaker and television personality, has now written over 300 books and sold nearly 200 million books over the world.

She has also had many historical works published and has written four autobiographies as well as the biographies of her mother and that of her brother, Ronald Cartland, who was the first Member of Parliament to be killed in the last war. This book has a preface by Sir Winston Churchill and has just been republished with an introduction by Sir Arthur Bryant.

Love at the Helm, a novel written with the help and inspiration of the late Admiral of the Fleet, the Earl Mountbatten of Burma, is being sold for the Mountbatten Memorial Trust.

Miss Cartland in 1978 sang an Album of Love Songs with the Royal Philharmonic Orchestra.

In 1976, by writing twenty-one books, she broke the world record and has continued for the following three years with 24, 20 and 23. She is in the *Guinness Book of Records* as the most prolific author alive.

In private life Barbara Cartland, who is a Dame of the Order of St. John of Jerusalem, Chairman of the St. John Council in Hertfordshire and Deputy President of the St. John Ambulance Brigade, has fought for better conditions and salaries for Midwives and Nurses.

She has championed the cause for old people, had the law altered regarding gypsies and founded the first Romany Gypsy camp in the world.

Barbara Cartland is deeply interested in Vitamin Therapy and is President of the British National Association for Health.

CHAPTER ONE
1898

"The letter has come, Mama!"

"What letter, Olinda?"

Lady Selwyn tried to sit up but failed.

Her daughter hurried to her side and deftly but gently lifted her mother higher in the bed and patted the pillows until she was comfortable.

It was a very sweet face, even though it was lined with pain, which looked up and said apprehensively:

"Do you mean in answer to yours?"

"I do, Mama. You will remember we read the advertisement together and decided it was something that I could do."

"They are sending you the work here?"

"No, Mama. That is what I wish to talk to you about."

Lady Selwyn's thin white hands clasped themselves together as if she anticipated she was to receive a shock.

Her daughter smiled at her reassuringly before she sat down on a chair by the side of the bed and said quietly:

"Please, Mama, do not get agitated about this before you hear what I have to tell you. You know as well as I do that I have to earn some money somehow; otherwise we will just starve to death."

She smiled as she spoke, as if to take the sting from the words, but Lady Selwyn gave a little shudder and Olinda went on quickly:

"You may not agree, but I think this sounds an excellent opportunity and I shall not be away very long."

"Away!" Lady Selwyn echoed faintly, fastening shrewdly on to the one word which Olinda knew would upset her.

Hastily she opened the letter which lay on her lap and read aloud:

Kelvedon House,
Derbyshire.

May 19, 1898

"Madam,

In answer to your letter of the 15th instant. I am empowered by the Dowager Countess of Kelvedon to inform you that she would wish you to travel here as soon as convenient to inspect the embroidery which needs restoration.

If it is within your capabilities, which it appears it would be from the Sample you have provided, Her Ladyship would desire you to start the work immediately.

The nearest Railway Station to Kelvedon House is Derby. A conveyance will be ordered to meet you there on receiving a reply as to the time the train in which you will be travelling will arrive.

Yours respectfully,
James Lanceworth,
Secretary."

Olinda finished speaking in her soft, musical voice and looked inquiringly at her mother.

"You see, Mama, I shall be working in a noblewoman's house, and the home of Dowager Countess of Kelvedon must be very respectable."

"But you will be employed!" Lady Selwyn said. "You will be treated as if you were a seamstress, Olinda!"

"That will be all the better, Mama!" Olinda replied. "I suspect actually I shall be placed in the same category as a Governess. That means I will not come in contact with the dashing, dangerous gentlemen you always suspect are waiting for me just round the corner!"

She gave a little laugh before she added:

"You know, Mama, if I listened to all your fears and anxieties about me, I should grow quite conceited!"

There was in fact every reason for Olinda to be conceited, except that she had no one but an adoring mother to pay her compliments.

She was very lovely, with large grey eyes in a small pointed face and hair the colour of ripening corn. She was slim and graceful and her long fingers, like the

10

expressions in her eyes, proclaimed a sensitive nature.

This showed itself in the gentleness and compassion she extended to everyone with whom she came in contact.

But actually her contacts with either men or women were very few.

For the last two years, since she had grown up, Olinda had devoted herself to caring for her sick mother and in fact seldom went outside the garden of the small Manor house where they lived.

It was an isolated part of Huntingdonshire and there were few neighbours to call on Lady Selwyn, especially after she had become so ill that she could only receive visitors in her bedroom.

The Vicar's wife was an occasional visitor, and so were several old ladies who lived in small cottages in the village.

Otherwise weeks went by when Lady Selwyn and Olinda saw no-one but themselves.

Olinda never complained. She loved her mother very deeply, but she realised that Lady Selwyn was growing very frail. Only expensive food could tempt her appetite, many items of which were beyond their means.

"We have to do something, Mama!" she had said firmly two weeks ago.

While Lady Selwyn had cried out in horror at the idea of her daughter trying to earn money, Olinda had said with practical common sense:

"There is no alternative, Mama. We could sell the house, but I doubt if anyone would wish to buy it. There was an article in the newspaper the other day saying properties for sale are a glut on the market."

Lady Selwyn did not answer, and Olinda went on:

"And if we did sell the Manor, where would we go? And it is not the house that eats up our money, it is the food we eat ourselves!"

"The food I eat," Lady Selwyn commented unhappily. "Do I really have to have so many chickens, Olinda? So many eggs, so much milk?"

"It is what the doctor ordered, Mama, and you cannot live on air or the few vegetables we grow in the garden."

She paused before she said:

"Of course we could dismiss old Hodges, but you know as well as I do he would never get another job, and Nanny never receives her wages anyway, except at irregular intervals."

"We could not do without Nanny," Lady Selwyn said quickly.

"Well, then, you have to consent to my finding some sort of work," Olinda said, "and as I am completely un-qualified it is going to be difficult."

It was Nanny who solved the problem of Olinda's capabilities by reminding her that the one thing she could do exceptionally well was embroidery.

"Perhaps if I embroidered some silk underclothes or muslin handkerchiefs like the ones I made Mama," Olinda had said reflectively, "I could find a shop which would buy them from me."

Lady Selwyn had given an exclamation of horror.

"How could you possibly go to a shop hawking the things you have made?" she asked. "I cannot bear even to consider it, my dearest."

"I was thinking," Nanny said, "that there must be ladies and gentlemen in big houses who require the embroidered curtains on their beds or perhaps even their pictures repaired. Do you remember, Miss Olinda, how skilfully you restored the picture belonging to your Grand-mama?"

Olinda had turned to look at it hanging on the wall. It was a very lovely example of the French 17th century woven in silk and metal-thread.

She had found it in the attic with a great number of things which had been sent to the house after her Grandmother's death, but which they never seemed to have time to sort out.

"How exquisite it would be, Mama!" she had exclaimed to Lady Selwyn, "if it were not so damaged!"

It certainly was a beautiful picture, representing the

12

figure of Summer holding a sheaf of corn and encircled with a wreath of roses, cornflowers, poppies and honeysuckle.

In the background there were garlands of fruit symbolic of the season entwined with small cupids and ornamented with birds.

Lady Selwyn before she had become ill had herself been an extremely clever embroiderer. She had been taught by her mother who was half-French and had been brought up in France.

It was Lady Selwyn who had taught Olinda that the art of embroidery had developed in France after the Crusades.

"Louis XI and Charles VIII summoned Italian embroiderers to France," she said, "and most of the exquisite work to be seen on vestments and altar fronts was done by Noble Ladies under the supervision of the ecclesiastical experts."

"How fascinating!" Olinda had exclaimed.

"In the eighteenth Century," Lady Selwyn went on, "Madame de Pompadour set the fashion for Tambour work, and the superiority of all French embroidery became so widely recognised that there was a demand for it in all other European countries."

"I can understand that," Olinda said.

"In the reign of Louis XV," Lady Selwyn said, "the designs had become gay, frivolous, and gracious. After the King's death, Madame de Mainteuor established a school for girls at St. Cyr where a great deal of their time was spent in needlework."

"Is any of their work still in existence?"

"Alas!" her mother replied. "Many embroideries of the Church and Palace were destroyed during the French Revolution, when the embroiderers were ordered to pick out the gold and silver thread."

"How petty-minded!" Olinda exclaimed.

Because Olinda was so interested she made her mother teach her the stitching she had been taught when she was young, and soon she could embroider as skilfully as Lady Selwyn herself.

When she was not reading she would sit making amusing patterns, which she evolved out of her head, for handkerchiefs or cushions or to recover chair seats which were, as she pointed out, all in need of new coverings.

At the moment Lady Selwyn was too frail to work herself, but she liked Olinda to sit beside her bed so that they could talk together while she worked and she was in fact her daughter's most severe critic.

There were many examples of Olinda's work in the house, but when it came to the point of sending a sample of it to the Dowager Countess of Kelvedon, it was difficult to know which to choose.

It was Nanny who had suggested that they look through the advertisements in *The Times* to see if there was anyone requiring embroidery in any shape or form.

"There might be ladies needing handbags," Nanny had suggested, "or a runner for the centre of the table."

"Or cushion covers," Olinda added. "They are easy to do, and I like copying the old designs that I have found in a book of Papa's.

The advertisement was in fact for a form of embroidery which she had not thought of before. It read:

"Lady of Title requires a Skilled and Experienced Embroiderer to repair the hangings of Period Beds. Write to The Secretary, Kelvedon House, Derbyshire."

"That means you would have to go to Derbyshire!" Lady Selwyn had exclaimed when Olinda read her the advertisement.

"I know, Mama, but I am sure for that sort of work they would pay well. I suspect the curtains will be either 16th or 17th century, and as you know I can do that particular embroidery quite easily."

"Why can they not send the curtains here?" Lady Selwyn enquired.

"Because they would be very bulky and very valuable," Olinda replied. "Besides, why should they put themselves

14

out? An embroiderer should be only too willing to go to them and, quite frankly, I would like to see Kelvedon House."

"Have you heard of it?" her mother enquired.

"I am sure it is a very fine and impressive house," Olinda said. "Somewhere at the back of my mind I feel I have seen a picture of it. Perhaps in the old copies of the *Illustrated London News* Papa kept. I will have a look through them and see if there is anything I can find out."

"Yes, do that, darling," Lady Selwyn said, "but I have not yet decided whether I will let you go."

Olinda put out her hand to lay it on her mother's.

"Do you suppose I would leave you Mama, if it was not an absolute necessity?" she asked gently.

"Are we really down to our last penny?" Lady Selwyn asked with a quiver in her voice.

"Very, very nearly," Olinda replied, "and there are another two years to go before we are clear of debt and your Pension will be your own again."

The two women were silent, thinking of the shock it had been after Gerald's death to find how much he had owed.

Olinda's brother, six years her senior, had been killed three years previously fighting on the North-West Frontier in India.

When they had learnt that he had died in a skirmish with tribesmen which was too unimportant even to be reported in the newspapers, something in Lady Selwyn had died too.

She had ceased, Olinda thought to herself, to go on fighting to live or to get better.

She had adored her son and although she loved Olinda, it was Gerald who brought a light into her eyes and who had sustained and comforted her after her husband's death.

There was a pension which had been just enough to keep Lady Selwyn in comfort, and on which she could have saved to give Olinda the clothes and entertainments which were her right when she made her début.

But after Gerald's death they found that not only did he owe a large amount of money because most Subalterns in India lived well above their means, but he had in a moment of mistaken generosity backed the bill of a brother officer who was in trouble from his creditors.

It must have been one of those coincidences, Olinda thought, that happen so often in real life but which people expect only to happen in books.

The very week Gerald was killed on the Frontier, his brother officer, who had been sent on a special mission to Calcutta, died of cholera.

The bill which Gerald had guaranteed, thinking presumably that he would never be expected to pay it, was then brought to his mother by the firm to which it was owed.

There was nothing Lady Selwyn could do but honour her son's commitment, and the only way she could pay off the bills he had left behind him was to mortgage three parts of her pension for the next five years.

It had left her and Olinda, they had thought, just enough money to struggle on at The Manor and pay the wages of old Hodge in the garden and Nanny in the house.

"We must be very economical," Olinda said, "but we will manage."

It meant of course that there were no new gowns for her and no chance, as her mother had planned, of her staying in London, when she became eighteen, with one of their relatives for a month or so during the Season.

She did not mind that, but as Lady Selwyn's health grew progressively worse, the special food which the doctors ordered for her together with her medicines, made it impossible to make ends meet.

The knowledge of their financial insecurity gave Olinda's voice a firmness as she said now:

"I shall go to Kelvedon House, Mama. But you are not to worry about me, and I promise you I shall work so quickly that I shall be back loaded with golden sovereigns almost before you realise I have gone!"

16

It took a great many hours of persuasion to make Lady Selwyn understand it was the only possible solution.

But finally Olinda had written back to Mr. James Lanceworth to say that she would arrive at Derby Station at 5 o'clock, Wednesday, May 30th.

When she was dressed for the journey, and the gown in sapphire blue batiste which she had made herself was covered by a travelling cape of the same colour, she looked so attractive that Lady Selwyn had reached out her hands to say:

"You ought not to go alone, Olinda! Supposing some .. gentleman makes himself .. unpleasant to you?"

"I will travel in a compartment for 'Ladies Only', Mama," Olinda said reassuringly. "And as for the gentlemen at Kelvedon House, I am quite certain they will be far too grand to look at a humble seamstress."

"I have heard tales," Lady Selwyn said in a low voice, "of Governesses being insulted in houses where they were working. Promise that you will lock your bedroom door very carefully at night."

"Of course, Mama, if you want me to do so. And, if I even see the shadow of a gentleman coming up the back stairs, I will lock myself in and scream for the Police."

"I am not joking, Olinda!"

"I know, dearest Mama. You are just worrying yourself over your small wee chick which is going out into the world all by itself. But have you forgotten I am nineteen and not a silly school-girl?"

She smiled.

"I shall behave with the greatest propriety and I promise that if there is any difficulty or unpleasantness I will come home at once."

"Do you swear you will do that?" Lady Selwyn insisted. "All the money in the world, Olinda, is not worth your being insulted or treated in a manner which would make your Papa angry with me for having let you go on this mad escapade."

17

"You make it sound a frivolous and luxurious jaunt, Mama," Olinda laughed. "I promise you it is just going to be hard work, but I am determined it shall be very highly paid and that is what matters."

She pushed forward her small chin a little as she spoke, and for a moment Lady Selwyn was reminded of Gerald when he wished to get his own way.

As usual when she thought of her son the pain of his loss was there and she was silent as Olinda went on:

"Nanny will look after you, Mama, and I have told all our friends in the village that they must come in and see you. Mrs. Parsons will read to you and the Miss Twitlets will take it in turns to arrange the flowers from the garden in your bedroom and do any shopping you may require."

She sighed.

"Everyone has been very kind. I expect when I get back I shall find you have not even missed me!"

"I shall miss you every minute of the day, my dearest," Lady Selwyn said, "and I shall not feel happy until you are back here with me safe and sound."

"And rich!" Olinda added as she bent down to kiss her mother.

She had however not felt quite so confident when she reached the Railway Station and found what a crowd of people there were waiting to catch the train to London.

It would have been impossible to make her way by train across country: the only practicable route was to take an Express to Derby from King's Cross, although it meant leaving Huntingdon at a very early hour in the morning.

Lady Selwyn had talked so much about the misadventures or the troubles in which she might be involved, that Olinda was relieved when she found herself safely in a second class compartment for 'Ladies Only' and the train left the great Metropolis for Derby.

It was then that the sense of adventure began to seep over her, and for the first time she felt excited rather than apprehensive of what lay ahead.

After all, it would be thrilling to see Kelvedon House because it was, as she had thought, one of the most important houses in England.

She had found a whole article about it in a back number of the *Illustrated London News*.

Kelvedon House, she discovered, had been built in the reign of Queen Elizabeth on the site of a Monastery.

The house had been erected in three stages, first by building on to what remained after the suppression of the monasteries by Henry VIII in 1536.

Then some years later it had been enlarged and made resplendent by the first Earl of Kelvedon who was Chamberlain to Queen Elizabeth I.

Finally it had been completed and became even more magnificent at the end of the 16th Century.

"It sounds very wonderful," Olinda had said to herself as she looked at the drawing of the house which ornamented the centre of the article.

Then she went on to read of the importance of its owner. He was, she discovered, 65 but he still held great posts at Court and was constantly in waiting on Queen Victoria.

A long account of his importance in the County followed, and at the end of the article it stated he had married Lady Rosaline Alward, daughter of the Duke of Hull, and had as issue one son.

Olinda turned to the front page of the *Illustrated London News* and found it was five years old.

'That means,' she thought, 'that the Earl must now be dead since the letter came from the Dowager Countess of Kelvedon.'

She put the magazine away and did not mention the present Earl, feeling that it might make Lady Selwyn more apprehensive than she already was.

She could not help wondering, however, how old the son might be. It seemed likely that he was about forty and therefore would not constitute the sort of danger her mother feared.

'Poor Mama,' Olinda thought, 'she still thinks we are

19

moving in smart society. She does not understand that poverty makes quite sure that one's station in life is a very low one."

As she packed for the journey it had not been a matter of choosing which clothes she should take with her but of taking everything she had.

They were all simple, plain dresses she had made herself, and she thought perhaps that if Kelvedon House was as grand as it had looked in the article it was a good thing that she would be confined to the back quarters.

There she would not encounter the fashionable ladies or the dashing gentlemen who would be entertained in the State Apartments.

At the same time she knew that that was where she would actually be working.

There had been a reference made to Queen Elizabeth's bedroom and the great bed in which she had slept.

There was another room that was known of as the "Duchess de Mazarin's Room" for it was here, the article said, that Charles II's mistress, Hortense Mancini had slept.

Because she had greatly enjoyed her visit, she had given her host and hostess magnificent French hangings for the bed which were still intact.

Olinda had brought with her a work-case filled with embroidery silks, but she was quite certain she would require a great deal more.

She only hoped that the Dowager Countess would be prepared to pay for them because they were expensive and she had very little money left.

She had taken with her only the minimum amount that she required for the journey and enough to tip the maids who would look after her.

She was sure they would only be under-housemaids who would not expect much.

At the same time it meant that she could not leave much for her mother, and she had already arranged with Nanny that the moment she received any remuneration

20

for her embroidery she would despatch it home immediately.

"It is an adventure!" Olinda told herself as the train gathered speed and she looked out onto the countryside bathed in sun. "I am glad I am visiting Kelvedon in the summer. The gardens will be beautiful and there will be so much to tell Mama about them and of course about the house also."

Her father had taught her a great deal about pictures and furniture.

He had never enough money to be a collector of beautiful things, but that did not prevent him from having an appreciative knowledge of them.

He had travelled to Italy and he had described to Olinda in detail the masterpieces he had seen in the Vatican and in the great Palaces and museums of Rome.

Because his daughter had listened to him attentively he had bought her books in which she could read of such national treasures, and even when she had been small he had taken her round some of the Museums in London.

'I wish Papa could be with me now,' Olinda thought.

Although he had been dead since she was fifteen, she still missed him because he had brought so much interest into her life besides imparting to her a desire for knowledge which, in the last years when her mother was so ill, she had had little chance to develop.

Occasionally she would go into Huntingdon on the Carrier and come back with a book she longed to read and on which she had expended her money rather than buy material for a gown or a new hat.

Fortunately the Vicar had quite a considerable Library.

Although the books were mostly old-fashioned and out of date, Olinda could borrow them as she wished and found quite a lot to interest her.

"But I am ignorant, very ignorant," she told herself. "What would Papa say if he knew what little chance I have of becoming better informed?"

There was no answer to this, except that now for the

first time she would have a chance of seeing a house that was part of history and could learn about its contents.

"It is exciting!" Olinda told herself again and again during the long journey, and when finally she stepped out at Derby Station it was like walking into a new world.

There was a smart liveried footman wearing white breeches and highly polished boots raising a top hat from his head as he came to meet her.

"Miss Selwyn?" he enquired.

"Yes, I am Miss Selwyn," Olinda replied.

"There is a carriage waiting for you outside, Miss," the footman said. "I'll see to your luggage."

He took her bag from her and ordered the porters about in such a lofty manner that her trunk was quickly brought from the Guard's Van and trundled outside the station.

The carriage was very impressive. Olinda knew it was the very latest design for a closed brougham and it was drawn by two horses.

She was handed respectfully inside and a light rug was placed over her knees.

Her trunk was strapped on behind and in half the time it would have taken had she been looking after herself the Porter was touching his forehead deferentially as they drove away.

Olinda bent forward to look out of the window at the town of Derby, but shortly they had left the houses behind and were out in the open country.

It was late in the afternoon and the shadows thrown by the sun were growing longer, but she could see fertile fields, thick woods, and every now and then she thought she had glimpses of impressive mansions behind long avenues of lime or elm trees.

She had an idea, although she was not certain, that Derbyshire was a smart county and that the gentlefolk who lived there were rich and important.

'Perhaps they will have Balls and Dinner Parties almost every night,' she thought and wondered what it would be like if she were travelling to Kelvedon House as a guest rather than an employee.

"You will not use your title," Lady Selwyn had said to her when she had first answered the advertisement which had appeared in *The Times*.

"Do you think it would be more embarrassing for me or for those who are to engage me that I should be an Honourable?" Olinda enquired.

"I would not wish anyone who might have known your father to learn what you are doing," Lady Selwyn had replied. "But Selwyn is not an uncommon name and unless you tell them, there is no reason for anyone to guess who you are."

"No, of course not, Mama," Olinda agreed, "and I assure you that Miss Selwyn, a seamstress, will arouse no curiosity!"

The Dowager Countess had at least been gracious enough to send a very comfortable carriage for her when she might have expected the type of open brake in which servants usually travelled.

She wondered what her employer would be like, and thought that since her husband would have been seventy if he were still alive, it was not unreasonable to think that she would be over sixty. Perhaps as frail as her mother.

Illness had made Lady Selwyn look far older than her fifty-four years. The loss of her husband and her son had taken from her the youthful joy of living which Olinda remembered so well.

Her thoughts of her mother were, however, swept away as the horses passed through huge ornamental wrought-iron gates and proceeded down a long avenue of ancient oaks which must from their girth have stood sentinel over the gravelled roadway for centuries.

Then just below them at the other side of the small valley there was a lake, and across it Olinda had her first sight of Kelvedon House.

It was even more magnificent and beautiful than it had appeared in the picture she had seen of it.

Its copulas, central spire and high Tudor chimneys were silhouetted against the deep blue of the evening sky and its long windows seemed to glitter iridescently as if they gave her a special welcome.

It was very large and very impressive; yet at the same time there was nothing frightening about it except its size.

Olinda had always thought whimsically to herself that houses had faces and the face of Kelvedon House seemed to her somewhat aloof, proud and dignified, and yet it had a warmth and a kindness about it.

She could see the great doorway in the centre of the building and the flight of stone steps leading up to it, but she was not surprised when the carriage turned to the left to stop outside a smaller, less impressive doorway.

Yet becaue she could not be received as an honoured guest in the magnificent house, Olinda, for a moment felt ridiculously disappointed.

"I shall be able to see the entrance hall later while I am here," she told herself consolingly.

The footman got down from the box to open the door for her and she was received by another footman who led her up a staircase to where a middle-aged woman, obviously the Housekeeper, in rustling black, received her.

"I am Mrs. Kingston, Miss Selwyn," she said. "Her Ladyship asked me to welcome you and show you to your room."

They shook hands and Olinda had the impression that the Housekeeper looked at her in surprise as if she had expected someone much older.

"You had a comfortable journey, Miss Selwyn?"

"Very comfortable, thank you," Olinda replied, "but I have been travelling since six o'clock this morning and would be very grateful if I could wash and change my gown."

"A house-maid will unpack for you," Mrs. Kingston

said, "and I'm sure while you're changing you would like a cup of tea."

"I would indeed," Olinda replied thankfully.

"When you are ready," Mrs. Kingston went on, "I'll inform Her Ladyship you are here. I expect she will wish to meet you, even though there will be no time for you to see your work until tomorrow."

"I am so anxious to know," Olinda said, "whether I am to repair the curtains in either Queen Elizabeth's Room or the Duchesse de Mazarin's?"

The Housekeeper looked surprised.

"You have heard then of our famous beds?" she asked.

"I have read about them in a copy of the *Illustrated London News*," Olinda answered.

"I expect Her Ladyship will want to tell you what is required herself," Mrs. Kingston said, "but I will be giving away no secrets, Miss Selwyn, when I tell you that the hangings on the Duchesse's bed are in urgent need of restoration."

"Oh, that is exciting!" Olinda exclaimed and thought there was a gleam of satisfaction in the Housekeeper's eyes as if she liked her enthusiasm.

The room which had been allotted her on the second floor was small but well furnished and her trunks were brought up by two footman, almost as soon as she and Mrs. Kingston reached it.

They were set down against the walls, the heavy straps were undone and the leather tops opened.

Then the men withdrew and two housemaids, who were both very young, in black dresses and white starched aprons with white caps covering their hair, knelt down to unpack.

"The Sitting Room which you will use is on the first floor," Mrs. Kingston said. "It is a small room that I have previously used for storing certain articles or furnishings that have not been required. But it has been arranged for you with a work table."

She paused to add:

"It is near enough to the State Rooms for you not to have to take half the day in fetching anything you might require for your embroidering."

She gave a little laugh.

"The house is so large I often think myself that it would be more convenient if we could have carriages to convey us from one part to the other!"

She paused to add:

"Or perhaps one of those new fangled motor-cars which I am convinced will only be a passing phase. Gentlemen will never give up their horses!"

"You have a car?" Olinda enquired.

"Her Ladyship has bought one for Mr. Hanson," Mrs. Kingston said. "A nasty smelly object I call it, and as it breaks down every half mile it is not likely he will get far in it."

She spoke almost with an vindictive note in her voice as if she was glad of the inconvenience.

Because she was curious, Olinda could not help asking:

"Is the Earl more interested in horses?"

"His Lordship is not here," Mrs. Kingston said sharply. "He is abroad and we seldom see him."

She turned to leave the room as she spoke, and Olinda felt that she had been indiscreet and perhaps presumptuous in asking the question.

At the same time it seemed strange that the owner of such a magnificent and historic house should not live in it. And who, she wondered, was Mr. Hanson?

By the time she had washed and changed her travelling gown for a plain dress of grey muslin which she hoped made her look a little older and more responsible, she learnt that tea was waiting for her in the Sitting Room downstairs.

The housemaid showed her where it was and she found Mrs. Kingston was waiting there.

Olinda saw it was quite a pleasant room with a window looking over the garden, and while there was a strong deal sewing-table occupying the centre of the room there was also a sofa and an arm-chair beside the fireplace.

The curtains were of a pretty chintz which reminded her of those that her mother had in the Drawing-Room at home and there was a thick carpet on the floor.

"I hope this is to your liking, Miss Selwyn," Mrs. Kingston said in a tone of voice which made it clear that she would be surprised to hear any complaint.

"It is very nice! Thank you so much. I am sorry to have put you to so much trouble in having to clear out the room."

Mrs. Kingston was obviously pleased with Olinda's politeness.

"It was no trouble, Miss Selwyn," she replied. "It is a good thing to have a clear-out now and again. I often think to myself that half the rooms in this place are the accumulated junk of ages!"

Olinda laughed as she was meant to do and Mrs. Kingston said:

"I will leave you to have your tea, Miss Selwyn. A footman will fetch you when Her Ladyship is ready to see you."

"Thank you," Olinda said. "Thank you very much for being so kind to me."

She was hungry after the journey. The cucumber sandwiches with which she had been provided were delicious and so was the madeira cake and the small rock-buns made with sultanas which she had not tasted since she was a child.

Nanny was not an adventurous cook, although she could roast a chicken to perfection and 'had a way', as Lady Selwyn put it, with an apple tart.

But cakes were not in her repertoire and, because her mother was not fond of sweet things, Olinda seldom troubled to make them.

As she drank the scented China tea she found her tiredness slipping away from her, and now the excitement was back and the thrill of knowing that tomorrow she would see over this great house.

She thought that the picture of its beauty as they had

27

driven down the drive would be etched in her mind for ever.

There was a knock on the door and when it opened the footman said:

"Her Ladyship will see you now, Miss."

Olinda rose to her feet, smoothed down her gown and followed the man down a broad corridor.

There was a green baize door at the end of it and when she had passed through it she found herself in what she knew was the main part of the house.

It was only a short distance before they came to the Grand Staircase, elaborately carved with each pillar surmounted by an heraldic figure. The walls were covered with pictures which took Olinda's breath away.

'If only Papa could see these!' she thought.

She hoped there was a Curator or guide who would explain them all to her and tell her who the artists were.

The Hall was as magnificent as she had expected. There were a great many marble statues; several fine carved gilt tables with green marble tops; and the ceiling was painted with a riot of gods and goddesses.

Olinda longed to stay and look at everything, but the footman was hurrying ahead of her and moving a little quicker than if she had been anyone of importance.

They reached two high mahogany door and the footman opened one.

"Miss Selwyn, Your Ladyship," he announced and Olinda stepped into a Salon.

It was so large that for a moment she was bewildered. Then at the far end she saw sitting on a sofa beside a carved marble mantelpiece, a lady who she knew must be the Dowager.

The long French windows all along one wall of the Salon looked on to a terrace, beyond which Olinda could see the garden and a fountain with its water sparkling in the evening sun.

It all seemed to dazzle her eyes, as did the mirrors which reflected each other and the huge crystal chandeliers sparkling overhead.

She had therefore walked the whole length of the Salon and reached the Dowager Countess before she could really look at her. When she did, it was with difficulty that she prevented herself from starting in surprise.

The lady on the sofa was much younger than she had expected and certainly did not resemble in any way her mental picture of a frail elderly woman, not unlike her mother.

The Dowager Countess of Kelvedon's brilliant red hair, fashionably dressed high on her head, was too vivid and too striking to be entirely natural.

She had also, to Olinda's astonishment, undoubtedly used cosmetics to darken the long lashes which fringed her green eyes and to deepen the colour of her lips.

She was beautiful: she must have been outstandingly, almost fantastically beautiful when she was young and Olinda found it hard not to stare rudely instead of dropping her eyes as she curtsied.

"How do you do, Miss Selwyn," the Dowager Countess said. "You are a great deal younger than I expected."

It sounded like an accusation and Olinda replied almost apologetically:

"I am sure I am not too young to do the work which is required, Ma'am."

"You actually did the cushion cover you sent us as an example of your work all yourself?"

"Yes, Ma'am."

Olinda had not been certain as to whether she should address the Dowager Countess as a girl of her own class would do, or whether she should use the more formal 'My Lady' as was expected of the servants.

"I am surprised, Miss Selwyn," the Dowager Countess said.

Her eyes seemed to flicker over Olinda as if she expected she was an imposter. Then a voice from the other side of the fireplace asked:

"If she can restore the curtains, Rosaline, does it really matter what she looks like?"

29

Olinda started because she had not realised there was anyone else in the room.

It was so large and so filled with furniture that she had not perceived as she walked towards the Dowager Countess that there was a man on the other side of the hearth.

Now she looked at him and wondered if he was the Mr. Hanson of whom Mrs. Kingston had spoken.

He was a well-built youngish man with a small moustache and bold eyes, which she felt were looking at her somewhat impertinently.

"I suppose not, Felix," the Dowager Countess replied. "At the same time it seems to me extraordinary that she could do such intricate embroidery when she can have had very little experience."

"Well, the proof of the pudding will be in the eating, will it not?" Felix Hanson asked with a laugh. "Put her to the test, Rosaline. If she can't compete with what you ask her to do, then she can be sent away."

Olinda felt as if she were a bale of cloth or a bundle of rubbish of which they were disposing, but she stood still, facing the Dowager Countess.

"Well, I suppose I must give you a chance," the Dowager said grudgingly.

"I shall be very grateful, Ma'am, if you will do so," Olinda replied, "and I am quite certain that I shall please you."

"You will please me if you work hard and finish the jobs that require doing as quickly as possible!" the Dowager Countess said.

Again there was that sharp note in her voice that Olinda had noticed when she had referred to her age.

"I understand that I am to start first thing tomorrow," Olinda said.

"That is right. Mrs. Kingston will show you exactly what is required."

"Thank you, Ma'am."

Olinda curtsied again and walked the long way back across the Salon towards the door.

It was only as she nearly reached it that she realised

Mr. Hanson had followed her and as she touched the handle his hand covered hers.

She felt the warmth of his fingers and because it was unexpected, she started. Then she heard his whisper almost beneath his breath but just loud enough for her to hear:

"You are very pretty, mind you don't fail!"

His fingers squeezed hers. Then between them they had opened the door and Olinda walked into the Hall with the colour flaming in her cheeks.

CHAPTER TWO

"This is the Queen's Room," Mrs. Kingston said, and Olinda gasped.

It was more fantastic than she had anticipated and she only wished that her mother could see it.

It was an enormous room with a beautiful gold-embossed cornice, and the walls were covered with panels painted with flowers and buds.

The great bed with its heavy carved gilt canopy was hung with curtains embroidered in a manner which she knew must be unique.

"It is beautiful!" she exclaimed.

"I thought you would think so," Mrs. Kingston said proudly.

Olinda had already learnt that Mrs. Kingston and all the senior servants felt that the treasures at Kelvedon House belonged to them almost as much as they belonged to the family.

It was in their blood, and Mrs. Kingston had told her that not only had she come to the great house to work when she was a child of twelve, but she had followed in the footsteps of her mother, her father and her two sets of grand-parents who had all worked on the Estate all their lives.

Her hair was now going grey, but her face was hardly lined. Yet she had an authority which Olinda was sure seemed awe-inspiring to the younger girls she trained under her.

"There is not very much to do to this bed itself," said Mrs. Kingston. "But now I think of it, there is a stitch or two required on one of the curtains."

She paused.

"Oh, yes, here it is! You will see that where the fringe joins the embroidery some of the threads have worked loose."

"I can do that here quite easily," Olinda said.

She was feeling almost bewildered with the beauties of the house, because Mrs. Kingston had started at the beginning when she showed her round the Great Banqueting Hall with its walls covered with murals painted by Verrio.

They were so lovely that Olinda felt that she could have stayed there all day long looking at the intricate detail of the artist's paintings and feeling almost as if the mythical figures he had depicted could walk down from the walls and talk to her.

The State Drawing Room was, Olinda thought, not so attractive as some of the other rooms.

Perhaps it was because one felt overshadowed by the huge figures on the tapestries, woven at the Royal Factory at Mortlake in 1635, after the celebrated cartoons by Raphael.

She wished however that her mother could see them, knowing she would have been thrilled with them, as she would have been by the Chinese furniture which one of the Earls of Kelvedon had brought back from China.

The lacquer cabinets seemed to fit into place even in an English home.

However the Library delighted her more than any other room.

Here there was a magnificent ceiling by Laguerre with gilded plaster work and she learnt that the room was actually used as a gallery until the beginning of the century.

She thought not only that it had a beauty and atmosphere, but the fragrance of ancient leather had an attraction all of its own.

It was when they came to the State Bedrooms that Olinda tried to forget in bewilderment the pictures, furniture, objets d'art, ceilings and murals downstairs, so as to concentrate on what would be her task here in this fabulously, unbelievably beautiful house.

Mrs. Kingston took her first to see what she called the Master Suite which had been designed by the original builder of the house for the 1st Earl of Kelvedon.

'He was certainly determined,' Olinda thought, 'to sleep as well as he lived.'

The huge four-poster bed was so high that it nearly touched the painted ceiling, and the head-piece was carved with the Kelvedon Coat of Arms which shone against the curtains of blood-red velvet embroidered with gold thread.

Carved and gilt wall mirrors displayed the Kelvedon Arms, and the landscapes painted round the cornice depicted different parts of the Estate.

The only modern painting was a magnificent picture of the Dowager Countess over the carved mantelpiece.

Looking at it Olinda realised again how outstanding she must have been when she was young.

Her red hair and green eyes against the transparent whiteness of her skin made her seem somehow even more alluring than the Venuses who rioted above her on the ceiling.

"Her Ladyship was very lovely when this was painted," Olinda said aloud.

"She was proclaimed the most beautiful girl in England when his late Lordship married her," Mrs. Kingston replied.

"I can understand that," Olinda answered. "And she is still beautiful now."

"We all have to get old," Mrs. Kingston said with a sharp note in her voice, "though some people find it difficult to accept the fact."

She paused and then said:

"I will show you Her Ladyship's room."

She moved towards a communicating door as she spoke and Olinda taking a last glance back at the huge velvet bed realised for the first time that the room she was leaving was actually in use.

There were ivory brushes on the dressing-table, a pair of slippers under an arm-chair and various small objects on top of the chest of drawers such as a wallet and a magazine.

On one of the arm-chairs a pair of riding-gloves must

have been thrown down since the Valet had tidied the room.

As if she realised what Olinda had noticed, Mrs. Kingston said nothing but seemed to hurry her along the communicating passage which led to the next room.

"The cupboards here were used by the Georgians as powder closets and now hold Her Ladyship's clothes," Mrs. Kingston explained.

She opened the door and Olinda stepped into another fabulous bedroom, this one decorated all in soft blues and pinks.

The painted ceiling depicted cupids rather than Goddesses, the furniture and the posts of the bed were all of carved wood covered with silver.

"How lovely!" she exclaimed.

She thought, as she looked round, it must be extremely becoming to the Dowager Countess's vivid red hair and green eyes.

"The bed-hangings were originally in rose pink," the Housekeeper explained, "but they were removed and replaced as you see, with a pale blue taffeta silk. So this room, Miss Selwyn, will not require your services."

"I am sad about that," Olinda replied with a smile, "because it is so lovely I should have liked to work here."

"I think you will also admire the Duchesse de Mazarin's Room where there is a great deal for you to do," Mrs. Kingston said.

Olinda was just about to follow her when she saw that on one side of the mantelpiece there was a portrait.

It was of a young man with dark hair and a handsome face. She had already seen so many portraits in the house and could not help wondering why this one arrested her attention.

"Who is that?" she asked.

"His Lordship, the present Earl, painted by Sargent," Mrs. Kingston replied.

"He is very good-looking," Olinda observed.

"He was a beautiful baby, and the most attractive young man it was possible to imagine," Mrs. Kingston said with a warmth in her voice that had not been there before.

"Does he live here?" Olinda asked.

There was a pause and she felt she had asked something indiscreet before Mrs. Kingston said in a very different tone:

"His Lordship has been abroad for the last two years."

"Without coming back?" Olinda asked in surprise. "How could he bear to leave this wonderful house for so long?"

"His Lordship doubtless has his own reasons," Mrs. Kingston said stiffly, and Olinda realised that indeed she had been indiscreet.

"I am sorry if I seem curious," she said hastily. "But the house fascinates me, and of course the history of its owners."

Mrs. Kingston seemed to soften.

"You must ask Mr. Thompson, the Curator, to find you a book telling you about the house and the history of the Kelvedons down to the present day."

"I read about the late Earl in the *Illustrated London News*," Olinda said. "It said how distinguished he was and how many important posts he occupied."

"He was a great gentleman, Miss Selwyn. We all admired His Lordship and were proud to work for him. It was a sad day when he left us."

There was no doubt about the sincerity in what Mrs. Kingston said, and Olinda could not help wondering whether she was disappointed with the present Earl.

At the same time there had been a warmth in her voice when speaking of him, which was unmistakable.

"There is something strange here," she thought to herself.

Then as they moved into the next State Room she could only give yet another cry of astonishment.

The walls of the Duchesse de Mazarin's Room were covered with tapestries depicting nymphs rioting in woodlands while the bed with its embroidered curtains was even more magnificent than she had expected it to be.

During the night when she had been thinking of Hortense, the Duchesse de Mazarin, Olinda had remembered her background and why she had come to England.

Hortense Mancini, one of the three nieces of Cardinal Mazarin, had been unusually gifted and besides being exquisitely beautiful, was one of the richest heiresses in France.

The Cardinal had chosen for her husband Armand de la Porte de la Meillaraye, who agreed that when he married Hortense he would take the name of Mazarin and the Dukedom that went with it.

She had brought her bridegroom her exquisite Italian beauty, an inexhaustible fountain of passionate love, together with the Cardinal's wedding gift of thirty million francs.

Unfortunately, soon after they were married her bridegroom began to show signs of incipient madness, and while he was infatuated with his wife's beauty, he fought against it because he believed that all physical delights were the road to Hell.

He began to find relief in religious ecstasy, which took the form of interminable and exhausting acts of repentance for his fleshly sins.

He would wander around the Palace intoning prayers, striking at priceless antique statues with a hammer and daubing black paint on the pictures which he considered were indecent.

Hortense bore her husband a son and three daughters in the space of seven years, but their father was so intent on stamping out the lusts that beset him that he ordered apothecaries to pull the front teeth of his daughters so that they should be ugly.

The Duchesse managed to prevent this happening and bore her appalling life with patience until finally she could stand it no more and ran away.

The Duc then tried to have her incarcerated in a prison-convent for prostitutes and fallen women.

He brought hundreds of indecent and foul charges against her, until finally after a series of bizarre and dangerous adventures she reached Rome. But she was to find no rest there.

Again and again she had to flee for her life to different parts of Europe, finally reaching the Netherlands and Amsterdam, and from there she set out for England.

When she arrived in London, King Charles II welcomed her in person. At thirty years of age, Hortense was one of the loveliest women Charles, a connoisseur of beautiful women, had ever seen. He was fascinated not only by her beauty but by her mind.

Charles at forty-five, tiring of life mentally, physically and emotionally, found in Hortense someone who infused him with a new vitality, new youth and new ideas.

For the first time he found that all the phobias, frustrations and yearnings that had niggled at his brain and churned his conscience with the eternal question of right or wrong, could be discussed with the woman he also loved.

To the King she represented a new horizon in his affairs with women.

It was not only her beauty that held him captive and aroused him to an ecstasy he thought he had never known before but her mind seduced his.

She made him think that for a brief while he had found the glorious, compelling, understanding, ecstatic love which he had sought all his life.

The story of Hortense Mazarin, when Olinda had first read it, had thrilled her because it had seemed to her so different from the other love stories she had read.

Here was not the capture of a beautiful woman by a passionate and masterful man, but a meeting of minds, of hearts and perhaps souls.

Looking at the Duchesse's bed it seemed to her she could almost see framed by the exquisite embroidered curtains a lovely oval face with a straight little nose, a splendid and intelligent forehead, and expressive curved lips.

All these combined with a brilliant intellect had

aroused within the King, a love he had thought would always elude him.

Olinda had stood silent for so long that Mrs. Kingston asked almost in surprise:

"You admire the bed, Miss Selwyn?"

"I have never seen anything like it," Olinda replied truthfully.

The embroidery of silver and gold thread, with the silks of every colour of the rainbow interspersed with huge pearls, was on black velvet. The headboard was an embroidered shell of silver executed in silk, depicting Venus rising from the foam.

Where Botticelli's Venus had been adorned only by her hair, this one wore a necklace of tiny diamonds round her neck and diamonds and pearls glittered in her hair.

There was hardly an inch on the black velvet that was not embroidered with birds and flowers and cupids and garlands, phoenix and stars.

It was a riot of colour, a kind of emotional ecstasy portrayed in needlework.

"It is quite wonderful," Olinda said at length.

"There are quite a number of repairs required on this bed," Mrs. Kingston said briskly. "The coverlet is the worst and when you are ready to repair it, I can have it brought to your room."

"Thank you," Olinda said.

"But someone at some time has torn the base of the curtain near the bed-table," Mrs. Kingston went on, "and that must be done here."

She showed the pieces that were damaged as she spoke.

"I think I have some silks in the right colours," Olinda said, "but I shall need a great many more."

"I was expecting that, Miss Selwyn," Mrs. Kingston replied, "and if you will write down exactly what you want, a groom can be despatched immediately to Derby to see if the silks are obtainable in the town. If not, they will have to come from London."

Again Olinda thanked her.

"This is really the most urgent repair, Miss Selwyn,"

Mrs. Kingston went on, "so I will not show you the other items for restoration until these are finished."

"That is a good idea," Olinda smiled. "I would not wish to feel overwhelmed at the start with what a lot of work there is for me to do."

"That is exactly what I feel when I am starting the Spring cleaning," Mrs. Kingston replied. "So I take a room at a time and somehow they all get done."

"I am sure they do," Olinda said.

She looked at the tear in the side curtain and thought it was not as bad as it appeared at first.

"Someone, perhaps by catching their foot in the fringe, had split the velvet up the side of the curtain for nearly six inches.

Some of the embroidery was damaged, some only frayed, and it would be easy to embroider over it and perhaps patch it at the back so that it would not be likely to tear again.

Mrs. Kingston looked at the watch that she wore pinned on her breast and which was surmounted by the initials V.R.

Olinda knew that it must have been given to her after a visit from Queen Victoria to Kelvedon House.

"It is your luncheon time, Miss Selwyn. I suggest that I take you back to your Sitting-room and that you return here after the meal and match your embroidery silks."

"I will do that," Olinda agreed.

"You will be able to find your own way?"

"I am sure I can. It is all on the same floor, although it is a long walk."

"It certainly is. I often think that if I measured the miles I walk every day in this house, no one would believe me!" Mrs. Kingston said.

"You have been very kind in showing me everything."

"Everything!" Mrs. Kingston laughed. "I certainly have not done that yet! There is the Orangery, the Armoury, the North Gallery and a dozen other places there has been no time to visit this morning."

"But I hope you will be kind enough to show them to me another day," Olinda said.

"I shall look forward to it and I am speaking the truth, Miss Selwyn," Mrs. Kingston answered. "It is not often I take anyone as appreciative as you round the house which, as I think you have guessed, is very close to my heart."

"Yes, I can see that," Olinda said, "and I think anyone who lived here would consider themselves very lucky."

She wondered as she spoke how the Earl could stay away for so long from the possession that must be almost unique in the whole world.

The article she had read about Kelvedon House had been right.

It was undoubtedly one of the greatest houses in England. There could be few Noblemen whose ancestral homes could even begin to compete with it.

As Mrs. Kingston rustled ahead of her, Olinda found herself thinking that whatever happened, she would never regret coming here.

The thought brought her back to Mr. Felix Hanson, and she knew that he had been in her mind a great deal since the moment that she had met him in the Salon.

At first she had only been angry at his familiarity when he had squeezed her fingers and whispered to her beneath his breath, then she began to think there was something about him which made her feel afraid.

It was quite obvious that he was the admirer and intimate friend of the Dowager Countess.

There had been a note in her voice when she spoke to him, and an expression in her eyes, that even Olinda, innocent though she was, could not fail to notice.

She thought now that nothing could be more uncomfortable than if Mr. Felix Hanson should choose to pursue her and make the Dowager Countess annoyed in consequence.

She could not have imagined such a thing happening, and yet there had been no mistaking the pressure of his fingers.

"I suppose this is what young women who are not ranked as 'Society' must expect," Olinda told herself.

She began to understand why her mother had been so nervous at the thought of her staying away alone.

She made quite sure of locking her bedroom door when she retired. At the same time she could not really believe that any man, if he were a gentleman, would approach a strange young woman in the house where he was an honoured guest.

At the same time her reading had told her that such things did happen and that unprotected women must expect men to behave dishonourably and in a manner which could, if it were discovered, quickly ruin their reputation.

"I will not be driven out of this house by Mr. Hanson, or by anyone else!" Olinda told herself bravely.

At the same time she felt a little tremor of fear, because she would not know how to cope with such a situation if in fact it arose.

Her first visitor, as she was finishing her breakfast in the Sitting-room, had been Mr. James Lanceworth, the Dowager Countess's secretary, who had written to her.

He was an elderly man with a rather precise manner and glasses through which Olinda thought he looked at her critically.

"I hope, Miss Selwyn, that you will be competent to carry out the task that awaits you," he said somewhat pompously. "I thought it only right that if Mrs. Kingston, and of course Her Ladyship, approve your work, you would wish to know what remuneration you will receive."

"Thank you, Mr. Lanceworth. I should like to know that," Olinda said.

"I have made enquiries as to what is the usual payment to embroiderers, and I must say that I find it extremely high, especially for someone as young as yourself."

"I would not wish to argue, Mr. Lanceworth," Olinda said, "but I cannot really see that the age of an embroiderer matters as long as the work she does is good.

A woman of fifty may be just as incompetent at coping with the intricacies of the art as she was at twenty."

Mr. Lanceworth considered this for a moment, before he said:

"I concede that point, Miss Selwyn, and therefore I am empowered by the Dowager Countess to tell you the accepted rate of payment which I understand for the particularly fine and exceptional work we require, is five shillings an hour."

It was with difficulty that Olinda prevented herself from giving a startled exclamation.

She had never in her wildest dreams thought to have been paid so highly, and only the self-control which was part of her upbringing made her say in a calm, quiet voice:

"That will be quite acceptable, Mr. Lanceworth, providing that my embroidery is to Her Ladyship's satisfaction."

"That of course, is the ultimate criterion," Mr. Lanceworth agreed.

He had then given her a brief bow and left the room while Olinda stood staring after him as if she still could not believe she had heard him aright.

Five shillings an hour! Provided she worked for six hours a day, or perhaps more if the daylight lasted, it would mean that by the end of the week she would have earned enough money for all the little luxuries her mother needed.

"We are rich," she told herself with a smile.

Then she remembered Mr. Felix Hanson and felt as if a shadow crossed her path.

* * * * * * *

When she had finished her luncheon, Olinda collected her embroidery silks and went along to the Duchesse de Mazarin's room.

It was with difficulty that she prevented herself from stopping every few minutes to look at an exquisite picture, a fine piece of furniture or a fascinating suit of armour.

She wondered if the people like the Dowager Countess, who lived in the house, really looked at their treasures as they passed by them.

Perhaps they were so used to the beauty of them, or their minds were so preoccupied with other matters, that the less important treasures in the corridors, on the stairs and in the Galleries escaped their notice.

Finally she reached the Duchesse's room and looked round her, entranced by the French furniture which had been added at a later date, but which toned with the bed.

The covers for the chairs had been copied, Olinda thought, about the reign of Queen Anne.

There were delightful inlaid commodes and a chest of drawers on which stood a mirror decorated with cupids in the Charles II manner. And there was a gilt stool supported by cupids, like the dressing table.

Hortense and the King must have been very happy in this room, Olinda told herself, and perhaps their happiness remained in the atmosphere.

She wanted to day-dream about Hortense and the handsome, cynical Charles to whom she had brought so much happiness. But Olinda told herself severely that she must get down to work.

The bed was set to the left of the door which led off the corridor, and there were three windows opening out on to the rose-garden below.

There was a scent of flowers coming in through the windows and the sunshine made a golden pattern on the carpet.

Olinda sat down on the floor and spread out her embroidery silks beside her.

Now she actually had the embroidered curtain in her hand, she saw she had been rather optimistic in thinking she had enough silks with her to repair even a few inches of the intricate pattern.

She would want, she knew, many more skeins of silk, and while she had some of the necessary colours she would require many more and a great deal of gold and silver thread.

As Mrs. Kingston had instructed her, she had brought a small note-book with her, and now she began to write down exactly what she would want. Afterwards she could copy it out neatly.

She must have been sitting on the floor for nearly half an hour when the door opened and she heard a voice speaking excitedly.

"I've been alooking for you everywhere, Mrs. Kingston. His Lordship's arrived!"

"His Lordship?" Mrs. Kingston queried. "Lord who?"

"The Earl, Mrs. Kingston! The Earl! He's just stepped into the house! He's with Her Ladyship now and, if you asks me, fur's agoing to fly!"

"I did not ask you, James, and you can keep your thoughts to yourself. But His Lordship never let us know he was returning."

"No, Mrs. Kingston, he didn't, did he, and he has brought a lady with him too. Someone, I don't mind telling you, who'll be a big surprise to Her Ladyship!"

"I'll go downstairs at once," Mrs. Kingston said in a tone of voice which by its very intonation rebuked the footman for gossiping.

"Perhaps she won't be wanting you now, just at the moment," the footman said tantalisingly. "Her Ladyship had sent for you before His Lordship arrived. But after I showed him into the Salon with the person as is accompanying him, I came upstairs to find you, as were my previous instructions."

"Really, James, I don't know whether I'm on my head or on my heels! Stop nattering and get out of my way. I'll go down stairs and see if Her Ladyship wants me. If she doesn't, I'll wait until she does. Is that clear?"

"Very clear, Mrs. Kingston," the footman agreed.

Olinda heard Mrs. Kingston rustle away and the heavy steps of the footman followed her.

She could not help feeling that this was most exciting!

The Earl of Kelvedon who had not been home for

two years had suddenly returned, and she had not missed the footman's reference to the lady with him, speaking of her at first in a disparaging tone and then referring to her as 'a person'.

She knew only too well what that meant in the servant's vocabulary.

Nanny and old Mrs. Hodges at home had varying descriptions of people who came to see her mother.

"There's a lady to see you, M'Lady."

"There's a woman asking to see Your Ladyship."

"There's a person at the back door."

How well she knew the way the caller had been summed up, and Nanny and Mrs. Hodges were seldom at fault.

What could be happening, she wondered, and thought it rather fascinating.

The portrait of the young Earl in his mother's bedroom had certainly been good-looking.

At the same time there had been a dark, almost Byronical expression in his dark eyes and the manner in which his hair fell against the side of his square forehead.

She wished now that she had had time to look at the portrait a little longer, but of course with any luck she would soon see him in the flesh.

Because she so seldom had anyone of her own age to talk to, Olinda had always told herself stories and invented fantasies which often became as real to her as reality.

Now she began to dream a tale in which the Earl came home and took over the great house and the running of his Estate, and that he brought with him an attractive and alluring woman.

Perhaps, like Hortense de Mazarin, she would give him happiness and they would fill the house with their children.

And so the saga of the Kelvedons would go on as it had in the past, descending from generation to generation and becoming in itself more and more a part of the history of England.

It is all so intriguing, Olinda thought, and wondered if the woman the Earl had brought with him was Italian or French.

If she was a foreigner, she would undoubtedly be disparaged by the servants, but that was not to mean that she was not in fact noble and perhaps even Royal.

There should be a Princess living in this house, Olinda told herself romantically. Then with a little smile she thought she was getting herself bemused with fairy stories.

Yet after all, what more fitting background than Kelvedon House for a fairy story?

She went back to her room and wrote down in her neat elegant hand a list of all the skeins of silks she thought she would require, then rang the bell for a housemaid to take it to Mrs. Kingston.

One of the young housemaids came hurrying in, looking most excited. She had already waited on Olinda at breakfast and her name was Lucy.

"Oh, Miss, such a to do!" she exclaimed. "His Lordship's arrived and the whole place is in a twitter!"

"I can understand that," Olinda answered, "because no one was expecting him."

"They weren't indeed," Lucy said. "And now Mr. Hanson'll find his nose out of joint, and a good thing too, if you ask me!"

Olinda did not know what to reply to this, so she said nothing.

"I've only seen His Lordship once," Lucy went on. "The day I came to work he left. But I've heard how fond everyone is of him on the Estate. Mr. Burrows the Butler'll be like a cat with two tails now his Master's returned."

"His Lordship has been away a long time," Olinda remarked.

"They thought he would never come back, Miss, and that's the truth," Lucy said, "especially after what he said before he left!"

Although she knew she ought not to gossip with the

47

servants, and that her mother would be ashamed of her, Olinda's curiosity could not prevent her from asking:

"What did he say?"

"He said, Miss," Lucy replied lowering her voice, "—and as he was in the Hall we could all hear it: 'I am damned if I will stay here under the circumstances and I will come back only when you come to your senses—if you ever do.!"

Lucy drew in her breath.

"And then, Miss, he stamps down the steps, gets into his chaise and drives off as if the Devil himself were at his heels."

Olinda laughed, she could not help it.

"Oh, Lucy you make it sound all very dramatic," she said. "Who was he speaking to?"

"Her Ladyship, of course!" Lucy replied.

She spoke as if she thought Olinda was being extremely obtuse not to understand what was happening.

"She comes out of the Drawing Room just as His Lordship was leaving the house. 'Do not go, Roque,' she says, putting out her hand. We were all apeeping over the banisters to see His Lordship go and she says it almost pleading-like, and that's what he answered her."

With an effort Olinda realised she should not encourage Lucy.

"It is all very interesting," she said coldly, "and now His Lordship must have changed his mind as he has come back. Would you be kind enough to give this list to Mrs. Kingston and ask her if I can have the silks as quickly as possible. It is really difficult for me to work without them."

"I will give it to her, Miss," Lucy said blithely. "But I doubt if she'll pay attention to you at the moment. She's running round in circles after His Lordship! But I'll do my best."

"Thank you, Lucy," Olinda said.

She took up her embroidery silks and went back along the corridors to the Duchess's Room.

She would have liked to go out into the garden, but

she told herself severely she had wasted many precious hours in the morning going round the house, when she might have been working.

Now if she was to earn money, she must settle down to work and remember that every five shillings was going to help her mother to regain her health.

The windows in the Duchess's Room faced South and had now lost the sun which was gradually moving round to the side of the great building.

It was cooler and as Olinda sat down again on the floor and took up the torn curtain she could hear the birds singing outside and smell the scent of the roses coming through the window.

"Could anyone have a more perfect place in which to work?" she asked herself.

She started to mend first the black velvet, darning it with tiny stitches so small they could hardly be seen.

As always when Olinda was concentrating on her work, she forgot her surroundings and everything except her own special innerworld into which she could escape with her thoughts and still work with her fingers.

She was thinking about Hortense de Mazarin and remembered that a contemporary had described her eyes as 'neither blue nor grey nor altogether black. They bore the sweetness of blue, the gaiety of grey and above all the fire of black'.

Charles II had found in them the secrets he had been seeking all his life, Olinda knew, and she wondered if any man would ever find the secrets he sought in her eyes.

"The gaiety of grey" was not really an apt description where she was concerned.

She had a feeling that her grey eyes were not gay but serious, and she thought they were perhaps a little dull. She was not sure. But how could one judge oneself and know what one's eyes conveyed to someone else?

The Duchesse was lucky, she thought, despite all the miseries of her married life, despite all she had suffered—eventually she found love.

Olinda glanced up at the side of the bed towering above her and raised her head to where the inside of the canopy depicted flying cupids encircling two hearts pierced with an arrow.

"A bed for love," Olinda told herself and realised she had looked up really because her eyes were hurting.

It was not surprising!

She had worked for so long that she had completely forgotten the time, and now the sun had long since lost its strength, the room was full of shadows and it was impossible to go on sewing any longer.

Olinda began to put her needles and silks back into the bag in which she kept them.

She had just reached out her hand for her long, thin, pointed scissors, when the door of the room opened. As it did so a man's voice outside in the passage deep and resolute said:

"Mrs. Kingston, I have been looking for you."

"I'm sorry, M'Lord," Mrs. Kingston replied, "I was just going . ."

Olinda realised she was about to say that she was going to the Duchesse's room to fetch her, the Earl cut her off abruptly:

"I want to know, Mrs. Kingston, what you mean by putting Mademoiselle Le Bronc on the second floor."

"On Her Ladyship's orders, M'Lord."

"Is that how you treat my friends when I bring them home?" the Earl asked and now there was a note of anger in his voice which was quite unmistakable.

"I'm sorry, M'Lord," Mrs. Kingston said again in a flutter, "but Her Ladyship said . ."

"I can imagine what Her Ladyship said!" the Earl said sharply. "You will change Mademoiselle Le Bronc immediately to one of the rooms on this floor. One of the State rooms, Mrs. Kingston!"

"Yes, M'Lord, of course, M'Lord, if that's what you wish."

"It is what I wish! My friends will be treated with

proper respect by everyone! Everyone in the house, Mrs. Kingston, is that clear?"

"Yes, of course, M'Lord."

There was a pause and then the Earl added:

"It was not your fault, Mrs. Kingston, I realise that. And, incidently, where am I sleeping?"

There was a silence which Olinda could not help feeling had something ominous about it.

Then Mrs. Kingston replied a little hesitatingly:

"I thought, M'Lord, you'd like to be in the King's room."

"Why not in my rightful place, Mrs. Kingston?"

"Of course, if that's what your Lordship wishes, I'll make arrangements immediately."

"I would of course wish to sleep in my father's room—in my father's bed," the Earl said speaking slowly. "That is where all the Earls of Kelvedon have slept, have they not, Mrs. Kingston?"

"Yes, M'Lord, of course, M' Lord."

She ceased speaking and then the Earl said violently:

"And throw that damned usurper out of there!"

Olinda heard Mrs. Kingston give a far from inaudible gasp and at that moment there was another voice asking:

"What are you saying, Roque? What orders are you giving Mrs. Kingston? I have already told her where your friend is to sleep."

"And I have countermanded your order, Mama. I realise quite well why you chose the second floor, but my friends, like yours, are entitled to the best!"

There was silence and then the Dowager Countess said:

"That will be all, Mrs. Kingston."

"Thank you, M'Lady."

There was a sound of Mrs. Kingston moving away, and then to Olinda's consternation she heard someone stepping into the room and the Dowager Countess saying more clearly:

"Why did you come back here, Roque, to make trouble?"

51

The Earl had obviously followed her, and now Olinda wondered frantically what she should do.

Should she reveal herself? If she did, they would realise she had already been eavesdropping. Before she could make up her mind, the Earl said:

"It is you who are the cause of the trouble, Mama. I have come back from France to find out exactly what you are doing in my absence."

"What *I* am doing, when you bring that creature here!" the Dowager Countess said, her voice rising. "I do not intend, Roque, to act as chaperon to one of your fancy women."

"My fancy woman, as you call her," the Earl said bitterly, "is on a par with your fancy man, Mama! I have brought Yvette to lend me moral support—or shall I say in an effort to make the foursome complete!"

"How dare you!" the Dowager Countess exclaimed. "How dare you speak to me like that!"

"How dare you behave as you have in my absence?" the Earl retorted. "But after all this is the reason why I went abroad."

"And you should have stayed there!" the Dowager Countess snapped.

"This is still my house!" the Earl replied.

"Have you forgotten, my dear son, that you cannot keep it up without money? The money that your father left to me completely and absolutely for my life time!"

"I have not forgotten that!" the Earl replied, "and do you imagine for one moment my father would have left you in such a position, except that he trusted you? With one word I could have destroyed that trust; but because I loved him, because I could not bear to hurt him, I allowed him to live and die in his Fool's Paradise."

"With the result, my dear Roque, that whatever you may say, I have the upper hand! If you throw me out of the house, then you cannot keep the place going. I hold all the aces, I think!"

"Exactly, Mama!" the Earl replied. "But the house is mine, and while it remains mine I will not allow your lovers, those young pimps who toady to you because you are a rich woman, to alter or deface my possessions!"

"So that is what has brought you back," the Dowager Countess exclaimed.

"Exactly!" the Earl agreed. "Lanceworth told me that you wished to change the Orangery into an indoor Tennis Court. I can hardly believe, Mama, that you have taken to tennis in your old age. It is therefore obvious who it is who wishes to spoil a perfect example of William and Mary architecture."

"It will be so much more expensive to build a new Court altogether," the Dowager Countess said.

"Perhaps you could go without quite so many gowns for one year. Or perhaps your lover without so many racehorses and an expensive car!" the Earl remarked acidly.

"What I give Felix is my business," the Dowager Countess snapped. "I do not suppose Mademoiselle Le Bronc, if that is her real name, is a cheap acquisition!"

"On the contrary, she is very expensive," the Earl said. "That is why I thought she would be such a suitable companion on this visit."

"Then you can take her back to the gutter where she came from," the Dowager Countess said. "I will not sit down to meals with such a creature!"

"In which case I will not sit down with Felix Hanson!" the Earl said. "What a delightful idea, Mama! Let us dine alone and quarrel with each other in front of the servants. An audience always gives such a piquancy to the type of interchange we have with each other.

"I will not stay here being insulted!" the Dowager Countess cried. "Keep your little French prostitute and she can sleep where you like. Doubtless it will be in your bed!"

"I might say the same of Felix Hanson, Mama. Except that I assure you, while I am in the house he will not sleep in my father's room however much he may try to take his place in other ways!"

There was a steely note in the Earl's voice which was unmistakable.

"I hate you, Roque! I hate you in this mood! Why did you have to come back? Why can you not stay away and go on debauching yourself, and trying to pretend it is my fault!"

"It *is* your fault, Mama, as it always has been," the Earl answered.

There was a long pause, and then the Dowager Countess said in a somewhat uncertain voice:

"Why do we not forget the stupid adolescent dramas for which you are now far too old."

She paused to add:

"You loved me so much when you were a boy. In fact you worshipped me! It was only jealousy that made you rage—and how you raged!—when you first realised I had taken a lover."

The Earl made a sound which might have been indicative of disgust.

"What else could you expect?" the Dowager Countess asked. "Your father was so much older than I was, and I wanted love, Roque! I could not live without it!"

There was an unmistakable note of pleading in her voice as she went on:

"Let us try now and be adult about this."

"In what way?" the Earl asked wearily.

"You could take your rightful place here."

"Would you be content, Mama, to be *alone* with me?"

Again there was a pregnant silence, until the Dowager Countess cried:

"Do you really mean alone? Do you really want me to grow old, to have no one to admire me but you? I cannot do that, Roque, I cannot! I want Felix! I need him! He is all I have left of my youth."

"And that answers your suggestion very completely," the Earl said coldly.

There was a little cry, the sound of people leaving the room, and the door slammed behind them.

Olinda drew in her breath with a gasp as she realised

54

she had been sitting tense and still to the point that it had been hard to breathe.

Now she rose slowly to her feet feeling ashamed that she should have been eavesdropping, but knowing it would have been impossible for her to interrupt and reveal her presence.

She was a little stiff from sitting on the floor for so long and as she rose she put out her hand to steady herself against the bed.

Then as she did so she realised that she had been mistaken. The room was not empty as she had thought, nor had both the people who had been talking left it when the door was slammed.

The Earl was standing at one of the windows looking out.

He could not have heard her move because she was standing behind the bed for some seconds before a sense of her presence infringed on his mind and he turned his head.

He looked at her incredulously. At her wide eyes a little frightened and apprehensive, at her fair hair silhouetted against the brilliance of the curtains, at her small hand resting on the bed-cover.

It seemed to Olinda as if neither of them could move, and she felt that he in fact was as shocked into surprise as she was.

Then he asked abruptly, his voice seeming to vibrate round the room:

"Who are you and what are you doing here?"

CHAPTER THREE

The Earl stared out of the window. The lake was molten gold in the sinking sun, the swans moving slowly over its smooth surface and the crimson rhododendrons were reflected in the water.

He thought how often he had dreamt of this particular view when he had been abroad. Always it had brought him an inexplicable pain.

Ever since he had been a child, the beauty of his home had moved him unaccountably, and at times when he was away from it at school or University it had been almost too poignant to visualise it.

Yet it had always been in the back of his consciousness, a part of himself, a part of his heritage.

He could feel the loveliness of it now, like a cooling hand on his hot forehead gradually soothing away the anger that an interchange of words with his mother had aroused.

Always Kelvedon could bring him peace and a feeling that the violent emotions that consumed him to the point of driving him away from home, were unnecessary.

"I love you," he wanted to say to the lake, to the arched bridge which spanned it, to the great trees centuries old which stood in the Park, to the green lawns sloping down like emerald velvet, to the water's edge.

And beyond the shrubberies which enclosed the gardens like protecting arms there were the high woods, in which when he had been a child, had dwelt Knights and dragons, and the mysterious supernatural beings who somehow also featured in the history of his ancestors.

He felt his breath coming more calmly. Then some sixth sense made him feel that he was not alone.

Instinctively he turned his head.

In the shadows that were beginning to gather in the Duchesse's room he saw on the other side of the bed a small pointed face with large grey eyes, framed by hair so fair that a ray of the sinking sun might have been left behind.

For one incredible moment the face which could have belonged to some nymph from the tapestry behind it, appeared to have no substance and to be attached to no body.

Then he realised that the woman or girl who was standing there was wearing a grey gown.

"Who are you?" he asked, "and what are you doing here?"

There was silence for a moment. Then a low musical voice replied:

"I am sorry . . I did not wish to . . overhear what was being . . said, but it seemed . . impossible to . . interrupt."

"Who are you?" the Earl asked again.

"I am an embroiderer and have been engaged to repair the curtains of the bed."

"And you were of course hidden while my mother and I were in the room."

"I . . am afraid so."

"And you thought we both had left the room?"

"Y.yes."

The grey eyes were very apologetic and after a moment Olinda said hesitatingly:

"You . . must be aware that I would . . never . . repeat anything that I . . overheard, and I will in fact try to . . forget . . it."

"I should imagine that would be impossible," the Earl said dryly. "But I accept your assurance that what you heard being said in this room will go no further. Will you tell me your name?"

"Olinda Selwyn."

"I am sure I can trust you, Miss Selwyn."

"Of course."

Olinda moved from behind the bed and the Earl saw she was taller than he had thought. At the same time she was so slim and graceful in her grey gown that he was not surprised he had mistaken her for a nymph.

'She is very young,' he thought, seeing the soft contour of her face and the long column of her throat which supported the head of incredibly pale gold hair.

It stirred some memory in his mind, but he could not think what it was.

She was moving towards the door and he spoke again:

"Have you been here long, Miss Selwyn?"

"I arrived last night. I am hoping that my embroidery will give satisfaction."

"Do you have to work?"

"Yes. I need the money."

She glanced at him again. Then she opened the door and passing through it into the corridor closed it very quietly, leaving him alone.

The Earl stood staring after her until as if it was an effort he left the Duchesse's room to walk along the wide corridor to the Master Suite.

He knew that when he reached it all traces of its previous occupant would have been removed, and in fact he found Higson, the old valet who had looked after his father, hanging his clothes up in the wardrobe and setting his riding-boots and shoes beneath them.

"It is nice to see you, Higson," the Earl said holding out his hand.

"I have been praying, Your Lordship would return before I retired."

"You are retiring?"

The question was sharp.

"There's been complaints, M'Lord, that I'm too old for my job."

"Complaints, who from?"

There was a pause before the old man answered quietly.

"Her Ladyship's guests."

"You mean one in particular," the Earl insisted.

Now the anger was rising within him again and seemed to make every word he spoke sound ominous.

58

"I'm afraid, M'Lord," the old man faltered, "I don't move fast enough for the gentleman, who's always in a hurry. Although His late Lordship and yourself, M'Lord, always said I'd no one to equal me with hunting-breeches, I finds it difficult to understand all the new fangled clothes that's required for motoring, for golf and a number of other games we never had before at Kelvedon."

"How old are you, Higson?"

"Sixty-three, M'Lord and good for a number of years more if things were like they were in the old days."

"Then you will not retire, Higson. Is that understood?" the Earl said.

There was a sudden light in the man's eyes that had not been there before.

"You mean that, M'Lord? But Her Ladyship said . ."

"I am the master of this house, Higson, and I will not have the servants who have served my father and me pensioned off until they are ready to leave. Besides I require you to look after me."

"You intend to stay, M'Lord?"

The question obviously took the Earl by surprise, and he walked across the room to stand in front of the mantelpiece staring at his mother's portrait before he replied:

"I do not know, Higson, and that is the truth."

"We needs you, M'Lord, we need you badly. We're not happy, none of us, without you."

The Earl turned round.

"What do you mean by that?"

"The stables do not like the new car, M'Lord. The horses are not much in use and the gentleman, when he does ride them, is not like Your Lordship."

"What do you mean by that?" the Earl enquired.

"He's hard on them, M'Lord."

"In what way?"

Again there was a pause before Higson said:

"Hard hands, a whip and sharp spurs, M'Lord, do not make a horseman."

"Damn it! I will not have that swine ruining my blood-stock!"

"It's not only that, M'Lord," Higson went on. "Her Ladyship is only interested in the race-horses these days. The hunters and the teams Your Lordship used to drive yourself are seldom taken out. It's abreaking Abbey's heart."

Abbey, the Chief Groom, had ''a way with horses' that was second to none in the whole county.

The Earl found himself remembering the thrill of driving his first Four-in-Hand under Abbey's instructions, and how when he brought them back safely to the front of the house his father had stood on the steps and congratulated him.

He could not have been quite fifteen at the time, he thought, and wondered if anything else he had ever done had given him quite so much satisfaction.

Perhaps it had been equalled when he was in at his first kill out hunting at the age of nine, and again when he had carried his own colours to victory at the Varsity Point-to-Point.

But it was Abbey who had taught him! Abbey who had made his father's Stud outstanding.

"You said that Abbey is dissatisfied," he said to Higson. "He is not thinking of retiring?"

"No, M'Lord, but he has had other offers, and a man like Abbey finds it hard, M'Lord, to carry on without appreciation."

"I will talk to him," the Earl said.

"He's been saying for a long time how much he wants to see Your Lordship," Higson said.

He hung the last coat up on the rail in the wardrobe and then said in a somewhat puzzled voice:

"What'll Your Lordship wear for dinner this evening?"

The Earl glanced at the clothes he had brought back with him as if he had never seen them before.

The Bohemian clothes that were the usual wear amongst those he associated with in Paris, the loose velvet

60

coats, the flowing ties such as he was wearing round his neck at the moment, the gauze waistcoats; would have made any tailor in Savile Row shudder.

Suddenly he saw how out of place they were at Kelvedon hanging in the wardrobe his father had used, and which had been placed against that particular wall in Jacobean days to hold the clothes of every successive master of the house.

"I came away in a hurry, Higson," he said. "I see that my man in Paris has not packed the clothes I shall need here. I am sure you have some of my old things stored away somewhere safe?"

"Of course, Your Lordship," Higson said with a smile. "Everything is clean and pressed and ready for Your Lordship's return."

"Then fetch them, Higson, bring them down and put them in their rightful place."

"Yes, M'Lord! At once, M'Lord!"

It seemed as if the Earl had waved a magic wand and Higson was twenty years younger than when he had entered the room.

The Earl glanced at the clock on the mantelshelf, undressed slowly, and then walked from his bedroom into the adjoining bathroom where his bath was already drawn and waiting for him.

There was a scent of verbena which was always used in the gentlemen's bathrooms at Kelvedon. Over the chair there was a great, white bath-sheet embroidered in one corner with his monogram surmounted by a coronet, and a bath-mat to match bearing the same insignia.

The Earl stepped into the water and as he began to wash he found himself thinking of the strange woman he had found in the Duchesse's room.

An embroiderer! He could not remember having met one before, but he could understand that one would be necessary at Kelvedon.

The Countesses of Kelvedon all down the ages had been skilled with their needle. There was one who had covered with her own hand-work the seat of every chair in the State Dining Room, and there were sixty of them, while her husband was away fighting with Marlborough.

And there was another, he recalled now, who had completed several exquisite silk pictures while the Earl of that time had languished in the Tower of London under sentence of death from the Protector of England, Oliver Cromwell.

The Earl remembered seeing examples of fine needle-work in the Louvre in Paris and feeling that he could equal every exhibit with what he possessed at Kelvedon.

"I hope to God," he said to himself, "that Miss Selwyn knows her job! I could not bear the embroidery, or anything else in this house, to be messed up."

This brought him back to the very reason why he had returned home suddenly and impulsively without even announcing his arrival.

How dare that impertinent upstart suggest altering the Orangery? How could his mother for one moment contemplate it? It was an outrage against good taste!

All the way on his journey from France to Kelvedon the Earl had found himself wondering frantically what else might have been defaced or altered.

Lanceworth at least had had the sense to write to him about the Orangery, but less fundamental alterations might easily have been undertaken on his mother's instructions.

Instructions inspired by Felix Hanson!

The Earl was scowling when he came from his bathroom to find Higson laying out the conventional evening-clothes that he had not worn for two years.

He had travelled almost round the world when he first left Kelvedon in a towering rage having told his mother she could choose between him and Felix Hanson, and that he would not stay under the same roof with her lover.

They had stormed at each other in a manner which the Earl knew was undignified but which the fiery temperaments to which both of them were subject had made inevitable.

He had remembered afterwards somewhat shamefacedly how he had always tried to emulate the calm, self-control of his father.

The late Earl never raised his voice, but made his disapproval felt even more effectively than if he had raged or shouted at those who had offended him.

But while the Earl adored his father and tried to emulate him, his mother's blood was also in his veins. Fiery, impulsive, sensual. The Alwards were noted for their uncontrollable tempers and their lack of emotional restraint.

They had figured in every scandal and in every social *cause célèbre* for the last five hundred years, and the Earl knew it was only by a miracle that his father had not discovered the way in which his wife behaved.

It was in fact only because he could never have contemplated that his wife would have a lower standard than his own, and he had trusted her inexplicably.

"You've not altered an inch, M'Lord," Higson was saying with satisfaction as he helped the Earl into his stiff white shirt and high starched collar.

"I had forgotten how damned uncomfortable these things are," the Earl said.

"But very becoming, M'Lord, and you look a real gentleman in them, if I may say so."

The Earl laughed as if he could not help it.

"Meaning that I did not qualify as a gentleman in appearance when I arrived. Well perhaps you are right, but when in Rome we must do as the Romans do!"

He took up a handkerchief and placed it in his breast-pocket.

"Does Miss Selwyn dine downstairs?" he enquired.

For a moment Higson looked puzzled, and then he replied:

"The embroiderer? No, of course not, M'Lord. She has her meals in her own Sitting room."

"Then we shall just be a very pleasant *partie carrée*," the Earl said cynically as if he spoke to himself and went from his bedroom aware that Higson was watching him admiringly.

*   *   *   *   *   *   *

Olinda was, as it happened, at that very moment, eating her own supper in her Sitting room.

Lucy had laid the table with a white linen cloth and there was a silver candelabra to stand in the centre of it. It was not a very elaborate one, it was true, but nevertheless it was a silver candelabra and held three candles.

While she waited on Olinda, Lucy chatted. This was something she ought not to do and Olinda knew that if Mrs. Kingston heard her the maid would be severely reprimanded.

At the same time, because Olinda was curious she made no effort to stop the words which flowed from Lucy's lips.

"Such a to do, you wouldn't believe, Miss!" she said as she served the soup. "The whole house is standing on its head, you've never seen anything like it! And Mr. Hanson turned out of his room! I'd like to hear what he had to say about that!"

Olinda did not speak and Lucy went on:

"But it was not right, Miss, it wasn't really. That's what we all said. The Master's room is the Master's room, and them that's not entitled has no right there!"

Olinda thought with a smile that these were not Lucy's words, but undoubtedly the sentiments of Burrows, the Butler, or perhaps Mrs. Kingston.

"Has Mr. Hanson been here long?" she asked tentatively.

"Over two years, Miss. They say he was the reason His Lordship went away."

Lucy went to the door. Another maid handed her the next course and removed the empty soup-bowl.

There was young chicken cooked with mushrooms and stuffed with *fines herbes*. There were several other vegetables, as well as two sauces.

Lucy was silent while she concentrated on handing them to Olinda, then she burst out again.

"There's nobody as likes the gentleman, I can tell you that, Miss."

"Why not?" Olinda enquired.

Lucy did not reply for a moment and then she said somewhat evasively:

"It's just the way he gives orders and—other things."

"What other things?"

"They're not things that I can repeat to you, Miss," Lucy replied.

She carried the food outside as she spoke leaving Olinda for the moment to eat in silence.

She was hungry, having missed her tea. Ordinarily she would have been delighted at having such delicious food and would have found it difficult to concentrate on anything else.

But now she found herself thinking not only of what Lucy had said to her but of the Earl.

When he had turned round from the window she knew that he was just as handsome as she had expected him to be after seeing his portrait in his mother's bedroom.

But in fact he differed from it so considerably that if she had not seen him at Kelvedon she would not have recognised him.

The portrait had been of a young man looking happy and obviously at peace with the world.

The face of the man who had turned from the window was dark, scowling and cynical in a manner which Olinda found it hard to explain.

He certainly looked disillusioned and perhaps to some people he would have seemed even debauched with the lines harshly etched from his nose to his mouth.

In fact in some ways he even resembled the portraits that she had seen of Charles II.

Once he had smiled at life; now she felt that he sneered at it and he had also in other ways, looked different from what she had expected.

She had never thought to see a gentleman without a high collar and neat cravat or tie round his neck. The Earl's collar had been turned down and he wore a flowing tie such as Olinda had seen French artists wearing in photographs.

His coat had been of black velvet and his waistcoat had a pattern on it.

She could not imagine her father, or indeed Gerald, dressing in such a way. Yet in some curious manner the clothes had become him, even while they had made him look Bohemian and even more Byronic than he had seemed in his portrait.

"It is strange, very strange!" Olinda told herself.

Lucy came back into the room.

"Oh, Miss, you'd die of laughing if you heard what's going on downstairs. Her Ladyship's sitting up as stiff as a ramrod at one end of the table and His Lordship glowering at her from the other! Mademoiselle de Broucy, I can't remember her name, is flirting with the two gentlemen!"

"What is that dish, Lucy?" Olinda asked, not liking to snub the maid but knowing that she should not listen to such tittle-tattle.

"It's strawberries and cream, Miss, with a special sponge cake in the centre. It's one of the Chef's specials. You'll enjoy it, you will really."

"I am sure I shall," Olinda smiled.

"And I don't mind telling you, Miss, that what you leave will not go back to the kitchen, not when me and Rose is about!"

"I hope I have left you plenty," Olinda said with a smile.

"Oh, we're not wanting you to feel like that, Miss. Have another spoonful, do!"

"I have taken all I want, thank you," Olinda replied.

"Mademoiselle is on the stage," Lucy went on, determined not to be circumspect for long. "She told Miss Woods, the Head Housemaid, when she was unpacking for her, that she could kick a plate held high above her head. What do you think of that, Miss?"

"Very clever," Olinda remarked.

Lucy brought her cup of coffee and set it down on the table by the fire-place. Then she cleared away what remained of the dinner.

"I'll leave the candelabra, Miss, until the footman brings up the lamp. They're a bit late tonight, but then as I told you, they're all of an upset!"

She left the room and almost before Olinda had time to sip her coffee she was back carrying a big brass oil-lamp which she set down in the centre of the table.

"That's better," she exclaimed, "you can see to read. But you don't want to do any more sewing, Miss, not after you've been working all the afternoon."

"No, I think I have done enough for today," Olinda replied.

"My mother always said: 'strain your eyes and you strain away one of your best assets'," Lucy said. "She's right, Miss."

"I am sure she is," Olinda agreed.

"Then I will leave you," Lucy said looking round to see that she had not forgotten anything. "I wants to find out what's happening downstairs! You'll ring if you want anything, Miss, won't you?"

"I will, Lucy. Thank you so very much."

Lucy shut the door behind her and on an impulse, which she could not explain even to herself, Olinda got up and locked the door. Then she crossed the room to sit by the window looking out over the garden.

It was very peaceful, rooks were gone to roost in the high trees; there was the cry of the night-owl and the soft coo of the wood-pigeons.

It seemed impossible to Olinda that so many passionate emotions should be raging inside the house when there was so much peace and beauty outside it.

"How," she asked herself, "could the Earl have brought

back such a woman as Lucy had described to Kelvedon of all places?"

But she knew the answer: he had done it deliberately to annoy his mother and to challenge her because of his loathing for the man she had put in his father's place.

She had only had a short acquaintance with Mr. Hanson, but Olinda knew that he was not the sort of man of whom her mother would approve.

There had been something in his voice too which had told her that he was not well bred.

It was not that he spoke with an accent. It was just something which jarred on her sensitivity just as it had been jarring to feel his hand on hers and his whisper in her ear.

"He will behave himself at any rate while the Earl is here," she thought reassuringly.

But her mind found it difficult to escape from the drama that was taking place downstairs.

Although it might seem amusing to Lucy, it undoubtedly was a drama.

The Dowager Countess, losing her youth and frightened of losing her beauty, was clinging to a man much younger than herself! Yet she apparently had the whip-hand over her son in that the money belonged to her for her life-time.

Olinda could understand the hurt of that to a proud, high-spirited young man.

He was the Earl, but he could not afford to keep up his possessions except with the approval of his mother. It must be an intolerable position to be in at his age.

She sat thinking about them for a long time. Then as she rose to put her coffee-cup down on the table she saw there was a piece of paper lying just inside the door.

It had not been there when she had turned the key in the lock and she realised that while she was sitting at the window it must have been slipped under the door.

Yet she had not heard anything.

It made her feel uncomfortable and apprehensive. She

even felt a sudden reluctance to pick up the paper and read what it contained.

Finally she did so and saw it was a sheet of writing-paper engraved with the address of the house surmounted by the Kelvedon crest.

In very small writing, almost as if the writer did not wish to draw attention to it, was inscribed:

"Fetch a book from the Library at 12 o'clock."

The note was unsigned but without the slightest doubt in her mind Olinda knew who it was from.

"How dare he!" she exclaimed to herself. "How dare he think that I would lower myself to meet him clandestinely."

Then she thought that if Mr. Hanson was capable of attracting the Dowager Countess, who had once been the most beautiful woman in England, he would not expect an insignificant embroiderer to be fastidious.

Olinda played with the idea of sending him back his note with a rude message on it. Then she knew that would be undignified.

'Let him go to the Library and wait for me!' she thought.

She tore the note into tiny pieces—so tiny it would be impossible for anyone to piece them together again—and threw them into the waste-paper basket.

Then she walked back to the window.

The peace of the evening had been disturbed for her and she could only feel herself seething with resentment at the position into which Mr. Hanson was trying to drive her.

"If I am not careful, the Dowager Countess will become aware of his interest in me and I shall be dismissed," she told herself.

It was not only the ignominy of it she feared, but losing the salary which would mean so much to her mother.

What she hoped to earn would not only buy all the immediate luxuries Lady Selwyn needed, but if she stayed a few weeks, Olinda knew there would be no great urgency for her to work for some months to come.

"How can I persuade this man to leave me alone?" she wondered frantically.

She felt as if he was encroaching on her, encircling her. With an almost childish fear she thought she could not escape from him.

He must have brought the note to her Sitting room, and if the door had not been locked he could have walked in and surprised her!

She thought in a panic that there was nowhere she could hide! Then she told herself that she must be sensible and keep her head.

Yet instinctively she looked over her shoulder, as if she expected more notes to be lying just inside the door.

"I am being absurd," she said beneath her breath. "One thing is certain, he will be conceited enough to assume that I will obey his instruction and meet him in the Library. For the moment I am safe!"

She had a sudden longing for fresh air and for exercise.

She had been cooped up all the afternoon working in the Duchesse's room and she had spent the morning going round the house with Mrs. Kingston.

Always at home she had walked in the garden and over the fields surrounding the Manor.

When her father was alive they had ridden together every day. And when her mother could no longer afford to keep horses, the local farmers, if they were busy, would sometimes ask her to exercise their animals on which they followed the local hunt.

'I must go for a walk,' Olinda thought.

She felt as if the rooms she had been allotted in the house were becoming a prison with Mr. Hanson lurking outside them.

Cautiously she unlocked the door.

The corridor outside was empty and she walked in the direction away from the baize door which led to the State Apartments.

She found after a little while, as she had expected,

the secondary staircase going down to the ground floor.

She guessed from the lay-out of the house that the passage on the ground floor led to the kitchen quarters and by taking her bearings intelligently she soon found a door which opened into the garden.

The key was in the lock, and letting herself out, she locked the door on the outside and put the key in the pocket of her gown.

'Now I shall be able to get in,' she thought, 'without anyone being aware that I have left the house.'

Outside it was that wonderful moment of dusk after the last glow of the sun has disappeared below the horizon. The sky was translucent and the stars were coming out one by one.

The moon was new, and because she wanted good luck, Olinda, once she was away from the house and in the shelter of the bushes, bowed to it seven times.

"Bring me luck," she begged with her face turned up to the sky, "that I may earn enough money for Mama."

It was not only the money she wanted. She knew if she was honest that she wanted to stay in this fabulous house with its wonderful treasures and absorb some of its atmosphere and history.

"There is so much it can teach me, so much I can learn."

She thought of the Library with its thousands of books.

"He shall not turn me away!" she added firmly. "I will not let him!"

She knew that ultimately the decision did not rest with her but with the Dowager Countess. If Her Ladyship even had a suspicion of what was happening . . .

Olinda drew in her breath.

Keeping out of sight of the windows she wandered through yew hedges surmounted by topiary work, through a Herb garden surrounded by Tudor walls of warm red bricks and into a lily-garden.

The fountains had been turned off and were no longer playing, but the goldfish were swimming lazily beneath the waxen blossoms and their flat leaves.

A small wrought-iron gate showed Olinda a path leading through an orchard of fruit trees which had shed their blossom, to where in the distance she could see the lake.

She had realised from the house that the lake was very big and very long.

As she drew nearer to it she could see that the walled gardens and great clusters of trees made the house almost invisible from this part of the silver water.

It was then she saw just in front of her a white building and for a moment wondered what it was.

She discovered it was a small Grecian Temple built on a small island in the centre of the lake and connected to the mainland by an exquisitely designed Chinese bridge.

The bridge must have been erected, she thought, following the lead of George IV who, when he was Prince of Wales, had made Chinese architecture and Chinese furniture fashionable by building his Pavilion at Brighton.

Its elegance and balance delighted her as she walked across it, feeling as if she was stepping into a fantasy which was accentuated by the perfect symmetry of the Greek Temple.

She guessed it must have been brought from Greece by one of the Earls of Kelvedon on a voyage abroad and re-erected here.

Perhaps it was at a time when so many of the nobility, like Lord Elgin and Sir William Hamilton, were collecting spoils from the Greeks who were too indifferent to their treasures to prevent their being acquired by noblemen with a love of the antique.

She walked round to the front of the Temple and found a small terrace.

From here there was a perfect view of the lake stretching away into the distance where she could just see the Adam bridge.

There was also a view of the house that made it from this angle seem even more like a fairy palace than it had when Olinda had driven down the drive.

She looked at the Temple and saw inside it there was a statue of two cupids entwined. It was too dark to see clearly, but she thought they must symbolise love.

She glanced up at the sky.

"I will wait until the moon rises higher," she told herself, "and then I will see it as it must have looked all those ages ago in Greece."

On the terrace there was a wooden seat and she sat down realising it had been placed at exactly the right angle from which to view the lake and the house silhouetted against the star-lit sky.

It was all so lovely, so unbelievably beautiful, that Olinda forgot everything that had been frightening her and found herself swept away into one of her imaginative fantasies.

She thought of Hortense de Mazarin arriving at Kelvedon House with Charles II beside her, both of them ecstatically in love and knowing that here in the country they could be closely together free from the stiffness and protocol of the Court at Westminster.

The Greek Temple would not have been here then, but perhaps they walked down to the lake hand in hand and saw themselves reflected in the still surface.

Each would have looked not at their own image but at the face in the water of the one they loved.

Then at night in the darkness of the great canopied bed they had been no longer King and a Duchesse, but a man and woman, whispering their love in a special Heaven of their own.

Olinda thrilled with the vividness of her own imagination. Then quite suddenly she realised she was no longer alone on the terrace.

While she was lost in her fantasy, her eyes fixed on the great house in the distance, someone else had crossed the Chinese bridge.

A man was now standing against the balustrade looking as she had done over the long stretch of water.

She felt her heart give a frightened thump, then realised it was not the man she feared it might be, but the Earl.

There was no mistaking the darkness of his hair, the breadth of his shoulders, and the shape of his head as she had seen it when he stood with his back to her looking out of the window in the Duchesse's room.

She did not move, she could only hold her breath, until as if once again he was aware of her presence, he turned to look at her.

Now the star-light and the first faint rays of the crescent moon touched the softness of her hair and revealed her wide eyes in her pointed face.

For a moment he stared at her incredulously. Then he smiled.

"Miss Selwyn!" he exclaimed. "You turn up in the most unexpected places."

"I am . . sorry," Olinda said nervously. "I did not . . realise this place was . . private."

"It is not," the Earl answered, "but I thought no one ever wished to come here except myself."

"I found it by accident," Olinda explained. "I went for a walk, saw the bridge, and the Temple looked so beautiful."

She paused, and he added:

"So you could not resist exploring."

"I have never seen anything so exquisite," Olinda answered, "and I was imagining how it must have looked when it stood in Greece."

She realised that her voice vibrated a little with the feelings it evoked in her and she added quickly:

"I will go now. I am . . sorry to have . . disturbed Your Lordship."

"As you were here first," the Earl replied, "the truth is that I have disturbed you."

He sat down on the seat beside her as he continued:

"Surely for a moment we can share both the Temple and the view of the lake."

"That is wonderful too," Olinda said. "I was thinking . ."

74

She stopped herself, realising it could not possibly interest him to know what she was thinking. But he said after a short pause:

"I am waiting to hear the end of that sentence."

"I . . was thinking," Olinda answered, "of the Duchesse de Mazarin arriving at Kelvedon with Charles II and how happy they must have been."

"Happy?" the Earl questioned. "It depends of course what you mean by happiness."

There was a sneer in his voice which was unmistakable.

"From what I have read about them at that particular time they were happy because they were genuinely in love," Olinda said quietly."

"How can you know that?"

"The Duchesse presented to your ancestor the curtains on which I am working because she had been so happy . . at Kelvedon."

"And in that bed!"

Olinda blushed.

"I want to believe," she said hesitatingly, "that the Duchesse at least for a little while gave the King what he had always sought all through his life."

"And what was that?" the Earl asked, almost as if he challenged her.

"Love," Olinda said simply. "The real love which had always eluded him and which yet he had continued to look for."

"Do you really believe that?" the Earl enquired. "Charles II, a roué, a rake, a man who seduced every pretty woman at Court! I cannot believe, Miss Selwyn, that you call that love!"

The Earl was speaking with a violence that told her that his own experience was involved in what he was saying.

Then suddenly she had a very strong desire to explain to him what she felt; to make him understand what she had imagined about the Duchesse de Mazarin.

She clasped her fingers together and looked up at the stars as if they might give her inspiration. She did not realise that the Earl was watching her profile etched against the white pillars of the Temple behind her.

However she knew he was waiting, and after a moment she said a little hesitatingly:

"I .. have often .. thought that true love is like the Holy Grail, which all men seek in their .. souls."

"And none find!" the Earl said harshly.

"That is not true," Olinda contradicted. "Many people have found it for a little while, but they have been unable to hold onto it. Perhaps that is what makes it so precious and which impels us to continue to search."

"What do you mean by that?" he asked.

"My father said once," Olinda answered dreamily, "that our ultimate ambitions should always be almost out of reach; that we must never quite attain them. If we did, the whole drive and purpose of our life would come to an end."

She paused and as the Earl did not speak, she continued:

"There must always be more to achieve, to conquer. Another mountain to climb, another horizon to seek, another guiding star twinkling overhead."

"You think it is possible to remain so optimistic, having failed again and again?"

"If we have brains and intelligence we can never be satisfied since we seek perfection."

The Earl was silent. Then he said, the mocking note again in his voice:

"You began by speaking of love. Surely you cannot expect such persistence of that illusory emotion!"

"I think love is divine," Olinda replied, "and everything within ourselves which is a part of that divinity craves for love, searches for it and yearns for it."

"Always to be disillusioned," the Earl remarked, and there was the same expression on his face that she had seen in the bedroom.

"Sometimes," Olinda corrected, "but that need not prevent us from trying again. That is what is so wonderful about love, it never comes to a full stop! There is always tomorrow, there is always another chance, it is never really too late."

"Who taught you these things?" the Earl asked sharply.

"My father died when I was fifteen," Olinda replied, "but we talked together about life. He loved beauty as perhaps other men might love . . a woman."

"That is what I was thinking . ." the Earl began, then stopped.

For the first time Olinda turned to look at him, waiting for the end of his sentence.

"How can I be talking to you like this?" he asked in a different tone. "We had not met until only a few hours ago."

Olinda felt as if he had suddenly struck a blow at her and the colour rose in her cheeks.

"I . . am . . sorry," she said humbly, "it was . . very impertinent of me. I must go back to the house."

She would have risen to her feet, but the Earl put out his hand quickly and caught her wrist.

"No please," he said, "I did not mean it like that. It sounded rough and rude, but it was only because you surprised me."

Olinda still sat at the edge of the seat and his hand was still on her wrist.

"Stay with me, please stay with me," the Earl pleaded. "I need desperately to have someone to talk to, and it is only because you frightened me that I spoke as I did just now."

"I . . frightened you?" Olinda questioned in surprise.

"Because you are here. Because you are different from anyone I have met before. Because when I first saw you I thought you were a nymph that had stepped down from the tapestry."

He gave a little sigh.

"I still think that you are not real and that at any moment you may vanish into the lake and I will never see you again."

Olinda did not reply and his fingers tightened on her wrist.

"Are you real?" he asked very softly.

"I . . am . . not sure," she murmured.

CHAPTER FOUR

The Earl gave a little laugh. Then he recited:

"A dream from the darkness of the night,
A dream from the stars and the gentle light
Of a crescent moon.
An illusion! A mirage false and a lie,
There is nothing in life but a death to die."

His voice seemed to vibrate across the water.

"I think it is being hurt that makes you feel like that," Olinda said gently.

"That is why I come here to delude myself," he answered. "Until now I have always been alone."

"I am . . sorry that I have . . intruded in such a . . private place," Olinda said.

"You know I do not mean that," he said quickly. "I feel it is right that you should be here—a dream I never expected."

She looked away across the lake and now the stars were reflected in the still water. The moon was growing a little stronger in the darkness of the sky and the twilight had vanished into the night.

"You were telling me about love," the Earl said.

"It was . . presumptuous of me."

"I am waiting to hear more."

She felt that, from being someone almost disembodied to whom she could speak almost as if she were speaking to herself, he had suddenly come nearer and become a person.

After a few moments silence the Earl said insistently:

"I want to hear what you think. You are in rather a unique position. You are a stranger and yet in the possession of intimacies which no stranger would know."

"I should have come out from behind the bed as soon as you entered the room," Olinda said unhappily.

"I can well understand that would have been very embarrassing."

Again there was silence until the Earl said:

"Perhaps as a stranger, and someone who would therefore not take sides, you could give me an unbiased opinion."

Olinda turned her face to look at him in astonishment. She could hardly believe that he was asking such a thing of her.

She could see his profile as he looked down the lake and she knew that his voice was undoubtedly serious and that he was in fact asking her for the truth.

"You might think anything I say was an . . impertinence," she faltered after a moment.

"Shall we say, tonight at any rate, that whatever we say to each other here in this secret place, we may give ourselves the freedom of the gods to say what we will and to expect no other response but gratitude."

"Which the gods seldom receive," Olinda smiled.

"That is true," the Earl agreed, "but as far as I am concerned I will listen to what you have to say believing it is a voice from Olympus and for the moment indisputable."

Olinda raised her eyes from the lake to look at the house.

Now many of the windows were gleaming gold and the moonlight just touched the cupolas making them shine in the darkness.

"It is so beautiful," she said softly. "You should find happiness there."

"I have tried," the Earl answered. "But the happiness I knew as a child could not stand up against disillusionment and the destruction of everything I revered and in which I believed."

The change in his voice was unmistakable and she knew that he spoke of his mother.

"I can understand how much it must have hurt you when you were young," she said.

"It crucified me," the Earl said almost savagely. "As it crucifies me now. She is my mother and the wife of

80

my father. How can she behave in such a manner?"

Olinda thought he would have said more. But he bit back the words as if he sought to control the violence of his feelings.

After a moment she said:

"Papa once said to me that when we judge other people it is always by our own standards, and that often prevents us from understanding them or giving them the compassion they deserve."

"What do you mean?" the Earl asked sharply.

"My father said," Olinda went on, "that we may denounce a thief; but how can we understand his action if we have never felt the compulsion to steal? If we have never starved or seen anyone we love hungry, ill and deprived."

She paused before she continued:

"He also asked when a murderer is condemned, how many of those who commit him with much righteous indignation have ever really been tempted to commit murder?"

"I understand what you are saying," the Earl said. "Of course I understand. But a woman is different."

"Every woman is different from every other woman," Olinda said. "But I think that all women even if they do not realise it, are also seeking the divine love instinctively. They too want to find the ecstasy and the wonder of it."

She paused before she continued:

"When they fail in their search, they accept second best."

"Can you be saying this to me?" the Earl asked. "Do you not know what I suffer from my mother not accepting second best, but third, fourth and lower still?"

His voice was savage.

"I know I am very . . ignorant of . . such things," Olinda replied, "because I have never loved anybody and no-one has ever . . fallen in love with me."

She gave a little sigh before she went on:

"But I know that for some women love can only be

81

expressed with their bodies, for others love is also of the mind, of the soul. That is . . real love."

She was thinking of Hortense de Mazarin and knew her words were hurtful to the Earl, but he had asked for the truth.

His mother could not face the fact that she was growing old and her beauty would no longer attract men. But she had nothing else to offer.

There was silence. Then the Earl said:

"Tell me what I should do, knowing the intolerable problem which exists in my own house—the house that belonged to my father and my forebears before him."

The harsh, bitter note was back in his voice.

For a moment Olinda thought how extraordinary it was that he should be speaking to her in such a way.

Then she realised that what she had thought about their both being disembodied had come true.

She was of no importance, insignificant, a nobody, and because of that he could speak as he would not have been able to speak to a friend or even to a woman with whom he was infatuated.

For him she was a dream out of the mists of the night, and therefore his defences were down.

He was asking her for help as perhaps he had never before asked another human being to help him.

"I think," Olinda said quietly, "you should come back. You should take your rightful place at Kelvedon and in the County. You should do what is expected of you."

"And tolerate that man living in my house, eating my food and degrading my mother by his attentions?"

"Each of us has to live our own life," Olinda said. "We cannot live anyone's else's. We should not really interfere with their development, their decisions."

"It is impossible!" the Earl said almost beneath his breath.

"I think that perhaps we are each something like the island where we are at this moment," Olinda went on as if he had not spoken. "The only real communication that we can have with one another must be by a bridge, and the bridge should be made of . . love."

The Earl did not speak.

He rose to his feet to stand looking over the lake. Olinda thought he was looking into his heart, seeing how useless and ineffective his anger had been in the past; how little his defiance had gained.

She did not know whether she had helped him or only made things more difficult.

She only knew she had said what came into her mind. It was almost as if the words had been there without her consciously seeking for them.

There was nothing more to say, nothing more she could do.

Rising she walked quietly away, moving behind the white Temple and crossing the Chinese bridge over the water onto the mainland.

She walked back through the orchard with its fruit trees, through the gardens. There was just enough light for her not to stumble and although sometimes the shadows seemed dark, she was not afraid.

She reached the house, let herself in and locked the door again on the inside before she ran up the stairs to her bedroom.

Only as she reached the safety of her own room did she feel as if she had stepped out of the mists of the night into reality.

"Please God, let me have helped him," she prayed as she got into bed.

She was still thinking of the Earl as she fell asleep.

✿　✿　✿　✿　✿　✿　✿

Downstairs in the Library Felix Hanson heard the clock on the mantelshelf chime the half-hour and kicked the fire-guard savagely.

"Damn the girl!" he swore. "Why could she not have the guts to come here as I asked her to do?"

The fact that Olinda had not joined him at his request he attributed entirely to her nervousness of being discovered.

Felix Hanson was extremely conceited because, ever since he had been old enough to realise that there were attractive women in the world, he had seldom, if ever, had his advances rebuffed.

It never struck him that a common little embroiderer who had come to the house because she needed money, would not be honoured by his attentions.

He was quite sure it was only a question of time before she would surrender herself eagerly, as a long line of similarly placed women had done before her.

In Felix's mind, the only difficulty was that the Dowager Countess was always on the look-out for such romantic interludes, so that he had little opportunity of pursuing another woman, however desirable she might be.

He had known that he was quite safe tonight, feeling that with the unexpected arrival of the Earl the Dowager Countess would undoubtedly be upset and certainly not anxious to flaunt their relationship in her son's face, seeing it was the reason which had sent the Earl abroad two years ago.

This had been in fact, Felix thought, an excellent opportunity to get to know the grey-eyed girl who had attracted him from the moment she had walked into the Salon.

She was just the type of woman he liked best, quiet, unassuming, modest and unawakened.

Doubtless, when he had remedied that deficiency, she would be like all the others, demanding, possessive and clinging to him, as he put it himself, 'like a piece of ivy'.

For the moment she would be shy, a little reluctant and entrancingly innocent!

He was determined that he would find opportunities of being alone with Olinda, however careful a watch the Dowager Countess might keep on him.

He kicked the fender again in irritation not only because Olinda had not come to the Library as he expected, but also because he was getting restless.

He had never before in his life had a *liaison* that had lasted so long.

There had been a great many advantages in being the *cher ami* of the Dowager Countess of Kelvedon, but he was beginning to think now that the disadvantages outweighed them.

Felix Hanson was the son of a solicitor in a small market town.

An intelligent man, Mr. Hanson had built up a good practice not only amongst the townsfolk but also amongst the country Squires, who found it more convenient and cheaper to employ him than a London firm.

Scrimping and saving, he managed to send his son, an only child, to a minor public school and afterwards to Cambridge University.

He had hoped that Felix might win a scholarship but it was soon apparent there was very little likelihood of that. However it was of course important, if he was to take over his father's practice, that he should get a Degree.

Felix, nevertheless, had an aversion to work.

He discovered that Cambridge could give him all the amusements that he had sensed were waiting somewhere outside the narrow world of the county-town in which he lived!

Soon he was part of the rich pleasure-seeking set of young undergraduates who were the despair of their tutors.

When he came down from Cambridge he had no Degree but quite an intimate knowledge of the fashionable world and an unshakable confidence in his ability to attract women.

He decided to exploit this latter talent and managed to do so with considerable ability.

He stayed in the houses of people his father would never have aspired to number among his clients.

He made love to any women he thought would further his social life and offer him the comfort which he found was indispensable.

He was, as a man who despised him said contemptuously, 'an Amorous Adventurer'.

Felix Hanson made up his mind that he would marry a rich heiress, forget his humble origins and move exclusively in the extravagant social world that he enjoyed.

The only obstacle was that the fathers of the heiresses were far more discerning than their wives and daughters.

Long before Felix got to the point of declaring his intentions, he found himself manoeuvred away from his prey, in a manner which told him all too clearly he was wasting his time.

There was however a profusion of attractive, young, married women, bored with their husbands and on the look-out for a flirtation or perhaps an *affaire de coeur*, with an unattached bachelor.

Through them Felix moved higher and higher in the social world and had actually on several occasions been included in parties where the guest of honour was the Prince of Wales.

It was on one of these evenings that he had met the Dowager Countess of Kelvedon.

Roseline Kelvedon had just emerged from a year's mourning.

She was bored with the country and the black crêpe in which she had been draped in the fashion set by Queen Victoria.

All the Balls and parties had been barred to her for what seemed to be an interminable period and she was determined to make up for lost time.

She was still extremely beautiful despite the fact that she was just past her 47th birthday, and her figure was that of a young girl.

She was also sophisticated, experienced with men, and more passionate than any woman Felix Hanson had ever known before.

To begin with he was swept off his feet and was, perhaps for the first time in his life, in love.

Even then it was a limited emotion because Felix was

too egotistical and too self-centred to be really concerned with anyone other than himself.

At first he made Roseline Kelvedon extremely happy until the rows with her son proved disruptive, and also her possessive jealousy made Felix progressively restless, but because she could not trust him she insisted on staying most of the time at Kelvedon.

Felix wanted the gaiety and amusements of London to stimulate and amuse him. He was not really a countryman.

He played the games he had learnt at Cambridge because they kept him fit, and he was always concerned lest the rich food and the amount of wine he consumed would ruin the athletic proportions of his body.

But Kelvedon itself got on his nerves. He had no appreciation of the house or its contents except that it gave him a feeling of grandeur because he could give orders to an army of servants and every comfort he desired was at his elbow.

Yet there was no point in having a car unless there was an admiring audience to see him drive it, in winning a game of tennis or going round the golf-course in under par without a crowd of attractive women to congratulate him at the finish.

"Let us go back to London," he begged the Dowager Countess all through the spring.

"What is the point?" she would ask. "You know you will have to live at your Club, or I could buy you a flat. It would be impossible for us to be together in the family House in Grosvenor Square, as we can be here."

"Why not?" he asked sulkily.

"Because my dear Felix, I should immediately be ostracised by every hostess in London. Do you suppose the Queen would not hear of it?"

Felix knew this was irrefutable.

He had thought at one time that he might persuade the Dowager Countess to marry him, until he had learnt that if she married again she forfeited all the money of which now she had the handling.

The late Earl had made a will when his son was still a small boy that on his death his wife should control the vast family fortune.

He believed that being so much older than his wife he might die suddenly, and Roque would not be old enough to administer the money wisely and sensibly without his mother's help and guidance.

He had always meant to change his will when Roque became twenty-one, but somehow the years had drifted past and he had not bothered to do so.

It was only when he was dead that the details of his will burst like a bombshell upon his son.

"How could my father have done this to me?" the Earl had asked himself a thousand times.

He knew the answer lay in the fact that his father had adored his beautiful wife!

The late Earl had never for one moment anticipated that she might behave in the manner which had shocked and horrified his son to the point where it embittered him and changed his character.

Roseline Kelvedon had been discreet and she kept to the Edwardian code of "never being found out" as long as her husband was alive. But after his death she had installed Felix Hanson at Kelvedon and defied her son to do anything about it.

"I have got to get out of here," Felix told himself.

He was not thinking of the great classical Library which he felt was yet another part of the prison closing in on him.

He would be twenty-seven next birthday and he told himself that if he did not take steps to settle his future soon he would find himself growing old, as Roseline undoubtedly was, with very little to show for it.

Like all women, she was prepared to give him expensive presents but kept him short of actual cash.

He had been wondering for some time how he dare approach her about his overdraft of over four thousand pounds at his bank and a bill of nearly a thousand about which his tailor was becoming increasingly objectionable.

The first thing, he thought now, was to get these paid off and then move out.

He had some small assets which would fetch enough money to keep him going until he found the rich wife he was seeking.

Perhaps he had made a mistake in considering young girls.

He had better find a widow who did not lose her money on remarriage, or perhaps a spinster whose not too obvious charms had left her unmarried until she would be glad of a husband, especially one as attractive as himself.

The world outside Kelvedon was full of opportunity, Felix Hanson thought. Yet here he was cooped up and Roseline getting more demanding, more possessive every day.

He knew she was frightened of losing him and decided that was the card he must play to get his bills paid.

In the meantime things were not as dull as they had been.

That little grey-eyed girl in the house was proving at the moment elusive but must obviously be brought to heel by the charm which only he knew how to use to its best advantage.

At the thought Felix smiled and caught a glimpse of himself in the mirror on the wall. He stood regarding his own reflection. There was no doubt he was exceedingly good-looking. There was no doubt too that women found him irresistible.

There was plenty of time yet for him to obtain everything he wanted in life, and a great deal more besides.

He was getting nowhere, wasting his time at Kelvedon.

"I will talk to Roseline about those bills at the first opportunity," he decided.

Then with a little swagger he turned from the mirror and walked from the Library, up the Grand Staircase to his own bedroom.

He was going automatically to the room he had occupied for the last two years when he remembered he had been moved into another room on the other side of the corridor.

It was certainly not so magnificent or so large, but for the moment Felix was not interested in furnishings.

He was thinking of his future and a very attractive pair of lips that he had every intention of kissing before he left the house.

In fact it was while he was thinking of Olinda that he fell asleep.

* * * * * * *

Lucy brought Olinda up to date with the happenings in the house as she waited on her at breakfast.

"His Lordship's gone riding, Miss," she said. "I heard Mr. Burrows say that Mr. Abbey, the Head Groom, was over the moon with excitement when His Lordship said the best horse in the stable was to be outside the front door waiting for him at eight o'clock."

"I expect he is a very good rider," Olinda said, because she felt some comment was expected.

"There's never been anyone like His Lordship, according to Mr. Abbey, and they say the horses've been eating their heads off for want of exercise. It is not the same being ridden by a groom, as when the Master is in the saddle."

Olinda was sure there was some truth in this, but she wanted to finish her breakfast because she wished to get back to work.

She was in fact just rising from the table when Mrs. Kingston came into the room.

"Good morning, Miss Selwyn."

"Good morning, Mrs. Kingston."

"I have just been looking at the work you did yesterday, and I must say, Miss Selwyn, I'm astonished to see how skilfully you've darned that tear in the black velvet. It's almost impossible to see where it was, and I am sure Her Ladyship will be delighted when I show it to her."

"Thank you, Mrs. Kingston."

The Housekeeper put a parcel down on the table.

"Here are all the silks the groom could obtain in Derby, and I've already despatched a letter to London to ask for the rest that you'll require."

"I have only asked for what I need for the Duchesse's room," Olinda explained. "When I see what else there is to do, I may want different colours, and I am sure more gold and silver thread will be necessary."

"I am sure of it and an exorbitant price it is too!" Mrs. Kingston smiled. "Things keep getting more expensive every year. I cannot think how we will end up if we go on in the way we are now."

"No, indeed," Olinda agreed automatically.

Lucy left the room and Mrs. Kingston said to Olinda in an almost conspiratorial whisper:

"I've to take that actress His Lordship brought here from Paris round the house this morning. It's not a task I'm looking forward to. I ask myself, what does someone like that know about antiques?"

"Perhaps she will be interested in the French rooms," Olinda suggested, thinking she would like to see Mademoiselle le Bronc.

"Yes, of course. I'll bring her to the Duchesse's Room. But do not be surprised when you see her, Miss Selwyn, she's not the sort of guest we're used to entertaining at Kelvedon House, that I can assure you."

Mrs. Kingston almost tossed her head as she spoke and certainly sniffed disdainfully when she went from the room.

Olinda could not help laughing, at the same time she could not help wondering about Mademoiselle le Bronc.

She knew the reason the Earl had brought her to Kelvedon, but that did not explain his close acquaintance with her and the fact that she was prepared to take a long and tiring journey because he asked it of her.

As she thought back at what had happened last night, Olinda was sure it must have been an insubstantial dream.

Now she could hardly believe not only that her conversation with the Earl had taken place, but that she had been so outspoken in what she had said to him.

What must he have thought of her discussing love with a strange man and, more intimately, his mother's liaison?

It was quite incredible that they should have sat side by side looking over the lake and talking of things which Olinda would have hesitated to discuss with another woman.

Yet at the time it had seemed entirely natural.

The words seemed to come to her lips without difficulty and they both had, as the Earl had said, the freedom of the gods.

But now Olinda thought it would be difficult to meet him again: she felt, if she had to see him face to face in the day-time, that she would blush self-consciously and feel extremely embarrassed.

"He is certain not to take my advice, but will go back to Paris," she told herself reassuringly.

But it was impossible not to think of him as she sat on the floor by the Duchesse's elaborate bed.

She stitched away at the embroidery which was frayed, covered a little flower with new pink and green silks, refurbished the delicate feathers of a bird and the wings of a cupid.

She was so intent on her own thoughts that it gave her quite a start when she heard Mrs. Kingston say:

"I'm sure this will interest you, *M'mselle*. This is the Duchesse de Mazarin's room and she slept here when she came to the house over 200 years ago with King Charles II."

"*Tiens!*" a voice exclaimed.

Then as Olinda rose to her feet she saw Mademoiselle le Bronc.

The actress was more flamboyant than she imagined any woman could be!

She had a piquant and gamin type of face with a large sensuous mouth, which, because it was painted flaming red, was the first thing Olinda noticed about her.

Her lashes were mascara'ed and her eyes had a provocative slant to them which gave her when she smiled an almost Eastern expression.

Her hair was dyed a coppery gold which was in direct contrast to the darkness of her winged eye-brows and made her skin seem a little sallow.

Yet all in all, the effect, entrancing and dramatic and at the same time complemented by a *chic*, was very French.

She wore a black and white striped gown with touches of red which matched her red lips, red slippers and red waist-band which encircled a really tiny waist.

On her head was an amusing little hat covered with red quills that no English woman would have dared wear with hair of that colour. Yet the whole ensemble was gay and alluring.

Mademoiselle le Bronc's eyes sparkled as she looked round the room and her mouth curved in a smile. The Earl, Olinda thought, had undoubtedly provided himself with an entertaining travelling companion.

"This is the Duchesse's bed," Mrs. Kingston said in the slow voice of a guide speaking to a rather obtuse child. "The curtains were presented to the Earl and Countess of Kelvedon of the day, in gratitude of the hospitality Her Grace received."

She looked at Olinda.

"And this is Miss Selwyn, who is repairing some of the embroidery that has been damaged during the passage of the years."

"*Bonjour, Mademoiselle,*" Olinda said.

"You speak French?" Mademoiselle le Bronc asked in the same language.

"*Oui, Mademoiselle,* but I do not often have the opportunity of conversing with a French woman."

"*Voyons,* then we must talk, must we not?" Mademoiselle asked. "May I see your work?"

She walked round to the side of the bed and Olinda showed her what she was doing.

"But you are an expert!" she exclaimed in French. "I was educated for a few years in a Convent, so I can sew—

93

the nuns made sure of that—but I could not do the work you are doing. It is exquisite! *Merveilleux!*"

"*Merci, Mademoiselle,*" Olinda replied.

Then because she was curious she asked:

"Are you enjoying yourself in England? Is this your first visit?"

"My first," Mademoiselle le Bronc replied. "Your country is very pretty, but it is not for me! I like Paris—the theatres, the Dance halls, the smell and the noise of Montmartre. It is too quiet here."

She said it in a way which made Olinda laugh.

"You will get used to it," she said.

"*Mon Dieu, Non!*" Mademoiselle exclaimed. "That is something I do not want, and besides I have my work, my career!"

"Of course you are an actress."

"A dancer, *Mademoiselle,* I dance at the Moulin Rouge."

She looked at Olinda and smiled.

"You would not have heard of it. It is not for nice girls like you. But it is amusing and for the gentlemen—what do you say in English?—'great fun'."

"And His Lordship enjoys it?" Olinda enquired.

"He is sometimes great fun when he is not thinking of this house," Mademoiselle replied.

She threw up her hands.

"*Tiens!* How he thinks and talks of this house! Kelvedon! Kelvedon! Kelvedon!"

She pronounced it in a funny manner.

"It is always in his thoughts, in his dreams and in his conversation!"

She sighed.

"I say to him sometimes, 'You love Kelvedon? That I cannot understand because it is not a woman. Women are there to be loved, women are warm, soft and exciting. Why do you think always of a house?'"

Olinda laughed because she could not help it.

"You make it sound very funny, Mademoiselle."

"It is not always funny for the woman who has to listen," she said. "*Milord* is very charming, handsome and enchanting when he wishes. But when he talks of Kelvedon he is very English and a bore!"

Mademoiselle almost spat out the last words.

Then she laughed and her red mouth seemed to curve delightfully and her eyes narrowed into mere slits.

Mrs. Kingston who could not understand a word of French looked from one to the other, until as if she felt annoyed at being left out, she said sharply:

"Now, *M'mselle*, permit me to show you the other State Rooms. They are all on this floor."

"I have seen enough," Mademoiselle le Bronc replied. "They are too big, too empty. They should be filled with gay people, singing, dancing, drinking."

She looked round her and almost as if she wished to be insulting, she said:

"In France we had the right idea in the Revolution. We emptied all the furniture out of the big Châteaux and burnt it."

"Burnt it!" Mrs. Kingston exclaimed in a voice that was almost a scream. "You must have been mad! The things here are worth thousands and thousands of pounds! And more important than money, *M'mselle*, they are each one a piece of history."

"What is history?" Mademoiselle le Bronc asked with a wave of her hand. "I want to live my own life and I'm not interested in other people's."

She turned to Olinda and said:

"And you do the same, *Mademoiselle*. You can sew when you are old, so live while you are young! If you ever come to Paris I will show you how to have fun!"

"Thank you, *Mademoiselle*," Olinda replied, "but I think that is unlikely."

"You don't wish to see any more of the house?" Mrs. Kingston asked with an almost incredulous note in her voice.

"*Non, Merci*," Mademoiselle le Bronc replied. "I am going downstairs to see if *Monsieur* has returned from exercising his horse, and then he can exercise me with a glass of wine! That is what I want!"

As she swept from the room, Mrs. Kingston looked back at Olinda and raised her eyebrows as if in despair.

Olinda found herself laughing as she sat down again on the floor.

There was no doubt about it, Mademoiselle le Bronc would be fun to be with, and yet even in her company the Earl could think only of Kelvedon.

There was something very pathetic, Olinda thought, in the idea of a man eating his heart away for the home he loved while surrounded by all the gaiety of Paris.

Then she told herself sharply she was being absurdly sentimental.

The Earl was not a pathetic boy forced to stay abroad because of some parental order! He was a man who had deliberately chosen to exile himself from his estate and his responsibilities!

He might have an excuse, he might find it intolerable to live with his mother under the circumstances.

At the same time he knew quite well where his duty lay and that those who lived on the estate relied on him. There was also his place in the social world into which he had been born.

"Perhaps I should have been more positive in what I said to him last night," Olinda told herself.

Then she thought it was altogether ridiculous to think that he would listen to her ideas.

He had talked to her on the impulse of the moment and because she was, as he had said, a stranger.

It had been night and they had both seemed enchanted under the stars beside the Greek temple. So they had talked as a man and woman might talk in a dream. In the light of day it had no reality.

"Remember you are just an embroiderer," Olinda told herself, but she could not help feeling her heart give a sudden leap as the door opened.

She was thinking of the Earl and thought that he had come to see her. She heard footsteps cross the room and then as they came nearer to the bed she looked up.

It was Mr. Felix Hanson!

For a moment she was not only surprised but quite ridiculously disappointed.

"Oh, it is you!" she exclaimed involuntarily.

"Yes, it's me," Felix Hanson replied ungrammatically. "If Mohammed won't come to the mountain, then the mountain must come to Mohammed! Why did you not turn up last night?"

Olinda bent her head over her stitching.

"You could not really have expected me."

"Of course I expected you!" he said. "I waited for you until nearly one o'clock. How could you be so ungrateful?"

"Ungrateful?" Olinda echoed in surprise.

She glanced up at him and found he was leaning against the bed-post in a nonchalant manner.

There was an expression in his eyes which made her look away hastily.

"If it had not been for me," he said, "you would have been sent home without a chance to prove your skill. You're far too pretty for this sort of job."

There was a caressing note in his voice and Olinda said almost sharply:

"If that is the truth, thank you. But now perhaps you will allow me to get on with my work. I have a great deal to do."

"I am delighted about that," he said, "because it means you will be staying for a long time. But I want to talk to you, little Olinda."

"My name is Miss Selwyn!"

"Olinda is far prettier and there's no point in our wasting a lot of time on the preliminaries."

"Preliminaries of what?" Olinda asked.

"Of getting to know each other very well. Very well indeed," Felix Hanson said softly. "Your lips attract me."

"You have no right to speak to me in this manner, Mr. Hanson, as well you know!" Olinda said.

"Who's to stop me?" Felix Hanson enquired.

"I cannot think that Her Ladyship would think it correct for you to be gossiping with one of her employees."

"She is not to know and therefore you and I have to be

97

very clever," Felix Hanson said. "We missed an opportunity last night that may not come again for a few days. At the same time, it might be possible for us to meet later this afternoon."

Olinda looked up at him.

"I have no intention, Mr. Hanson, of meeting you or seeing you at any time!"

She spoke clearly and positively, but he merely smiled.

"So you are going to play hard to get?" he said softly. "Well, a little reluctance always makes the chase worthwhile."

"There will be no chase!" Olinda said sharply. "If you continue to make such suggestions, Mr. Hanson, I shall go immediately to Her Ladyship to tell her that you are obstructing me in my work!"

She thought the threat might disturb him. Instead he threw back his head and laughed. The sound echoed through the bedroom.

"I like your spirit, Olinda. But I'm well aware, as you are, that you'll do nothing of the sort."

"I will if you do not leave me alone!"

"And find yourself outside the back door as quickly as you can pack your bags?" he asked.

He laughed again.

"Make no mistake, Her Ladyship knows very well which way the dice throw, and it is you who are expendable, Olinda, not me!"

Olinda was sure this was true. She pressed her lips together and went on sewing.

"So after that little skirmish," Felix Hanson said, "in which you must admit that I am undoubtedly the winner, let's begin to talk sensibly."

"There is nothing to talk about," Olinda said.

"I have a lot to say, although a kiss would express my feelings far better than all the words in the dictionary!"

Olinda put the edge of the curtain down in her lap.

"Listen, Mr. Hanson," she said. "I am here because I need the money. My mother is ill and only by taking this sort of work can I provide her with the food and medicine which will keep her alive. I do not wish to jeopardise my mother's health by philandering with you or anyone else. Please leave me alone!"

Felix Hanson laughed again.

"Splendid!" he said. "Act two, the innocent maiden to the wicked Baron who holds the mortgage on the house! My dear, you would make your fortune on the stage!"

"What I am saying is true, Mr. Hanson, and I am sincere!" Olinda protested.

"Indeed I believe every word of it, but I also know that I find you quite adorable and I intend to have those kisses sooner or later, however difficult you may try to make it for me."

He took a step nearer to her as he spoke and Olinda looked up at him apprehensively.

She felt he would find it difficult to kiss her as she was sitting on the ground, but at the same time her heart had begun to thump in a frightened manner and her mouth felt dry.

"Come along, my Sweet," he said in a voice that most women found irresistible. "We are now at the end of Act II."

He put his arms down towards her as he spoke and Olinda realised he intended to pick her up off the floor.

She moved backwards against the curtain and as she did so she picked up from her lap her long pointed embroidery scissors.

Felix Hanson's right hand was just about to touch her when she stabbed him with the scissors. The sharp point passed through the skin just above the thumb.

He gave a cry of pain and straightened himself, putting his hand to his mouth.

"You little vixen!"

He sucked his own blood for some seconds looking down at her angrily, and then perhaps because of the fear in her eyes and the fact that she seemed so small and ineffectual sitting on the floor. His expression changed.

"You will get into trouble, Olinda, if you go about behaving like that," he said. "Suppose I told her Ladyship that you are dangerous and it's a mistake to keep you here?"

"You would then have to explain why you were near enough for me to injure you!" Olinda retorted.

"You have an answer to everything, but I don't intend to give up so easily. As I have said before, I like a woman who is spirited."

He paused.

"It'll be amusing to conquer you, Olinda, to make you love me because you can't help yourself."

"I will never love you! Never!" Olinda replied. "And what you are suggesting is not love at all!"

"How do you know if you have never tried it?" he asked. "I would stake my reputation that you have never been made love to by a man. And I would not be surprised if you've never even been kissed!"

Despite herself the colour rose in Olinda's face.

"I was sure of it!" Felix Hanson said softly, "and I can assure you that no one can teach you better than I can the delights you are missing."

"I am missing nothing except privacy," Olinda snapped.

Felix Hanson sucked again his hand from which the blood was oozing.

"You intrigue me," he said, "and you have challenged me. It is a challenge I shall not refuse!"

"I have only asked you to leave me alone," she said breathlessly.

"Something I have no intention of doing," he replied, "and we shall see who will win!"

He walked across the room towards the door. Just as he reached it, it opened.

"Felix, what are you doing here?" a voice asked sharply.

Olinda knew who was speaking. It was the Dowager Countess.

CHAPTER FIVE

There was a perceptible pause before Felix Hanson said:

"I came in here to get a towel for my hand. Look!"

He must have held out his hand to the Dowager Countess who asked sharply:

"What has happened? What have you done to it?"

"Find me something to put on it," he said. "It hurts, I can tell you!"

He walked through the door as he spoke taking the Dowager Countess by the arm and leading her back into the corridor. Their voices died away in the distance and Olinda felt herself relax.

She had thought for one desperate moment there was going to be a scene in which she would have been involved, but she had the feeling that Felix Hanson was now in command of the situation.

"Why can he not leave me alone?" she asked, feeling that every moment she was in the house with him she was in danger.

"How did you hurt yourself?" the Dowager Countess was asking as Felix led her down the corridor.

"I tripped and fell against one of the suits of armour," he replied. "I can't think why you have them standing about in the corridor! My hand's damned painful, I can tell you that!"

"Why did you go into that room?" the Dowager Countess enquired. "Mrs. Kingston asked me to look at the embroidery that girl is doing and I find you there!"

The Dowager Countess's green eyes were suspicious as they looked up at him.

"What girl? What are you talking about?" Felix Hanson enquired.

"The girl you were so insistent should repair the curtains," the Dowager Countess replied, "and if she is in the Duchesse's room, as Mrs. Kingston told me, I cannot believe that you did not see her."

"I saw no one!" Felix Hanson said firmly. "I went in, as I've told you, to find a towel. My hand was bleeding! I opened the first door I came to!"

He sucked at his wound before he went on:

"Of course, as no one was sleeping there, there was no towel nor any water and I think my hand should be washed."

"I want to believe you, Felix," the Dowager Countess said.

"And why the hell shouldn't you?" Felix Hanson asked aggressively. "Good God! If I can't look for a towel and a drop of water without being cross-examined as if I were in the Old Bailey, life is not worth living!"

He spoke angrily. By this time they had reached the room in which he was sleeping and he walked in first, leaving the Dowager Countess to follow him.

He went to the wash-stand and poured some cold water from a china urn into the basin and put his hand in it.

"I suppose you've got a bandage?"

"Yes, of course," the Dowager Countess answered.

She left him to go to her own room and when he was alone, Felix Hanson gave a sigh of relief.

That was a near shave!

He knew only too well how Roseline would have behaved if she had found him round the side of the bed talking to the little Selwyn wench, let alone if he'd been doing anything else!

'Living here,' he thought to himself, 'is like living in an open cage.'

There was always somebody watching: he could not speak without feeling he was being overheard or do anything without being aware that Roseline was watching him.

'I've got to get back to London,' he thought to himself.

There was a calculating look in his eyes when the Dowager Countess came back into the room with some lint, a bandage and a bottle of antiseptic.

"It's not bleeding so much now."

Felix took his hand out of the basin and dried it on a linen towel.

"I am afraid this is going to hurt," she said as she soaked a piece of cotton wool from the bottle of antiseptic, then dabbed it onto the wound.

"God! You're right!" Felix exclaimed. "It does!"

"It will prevent any infection," she said. "The suits of armour are centuries old and you do not wish to have a poisoned hand."

Felix had the idea that the embroidery scissors with which Olinda had stabbed him would be clean and very unlikely to cause any infection.

But he could only submit with good grace as the Dowager Countess applied the lint and then a narrow bandage over his hand.

"If it gets worse," she said, "we will send for the doctor."

"I'll be all right!"

She finished tying the bandage before she said:

"I still cannot understand why you went in to the Duchesse's room. Why did you not come to find me?"

"Oh, good God, Roseline!" Felix ejaculated. "Must you go on harping on the same subject!"

"If I thought you were pursuing that girl as you pursued my trainer's daughter at Newmarket, I would throw you out, here and now!" the Dowager Countess said in a low voice. "I will not go through that humiliation all over again!"

Felix knew that when Roseline Kelvedon spoke in a controlled voice she was far more dangerous than when she raged at him.

"You were mistaken in what you thought then," he retorted, "just as you're mistaken in what you're insinuating now. Anyway, there's no need for you to throw me out, Roseline. I'm going anyway!"

"Whatever do you mean?"

"I'm leaving Kelvedon. "I have to go to London."

"But why? Why? What is happening?" she asked.

Now there was a very different expression in her green eyes.

"I have to find myself a job," Felix answered. "I need money."

"Why? What for? I give you everything you want!"

"You've been very generous," he said, "and you know how grateful I am. But I can't expect you to pay my debts."

"Debts! What debts?" the Dowager Countess enquired. "How can you need anything I have not given you?"

"Your presents have meant a great deal to me," Felix smiled. "No one could have been kinder and more generous in every way, but unfortunately my Bank Manager can't be paid with kisses!"

"You owe your Bank money?"

"I've been in debt ever since I was at Cambridge," Felix answered truthfully, "and now it's got to the point when they insist that I pay off my over-draft. And there are other debts as well."

The Dowager Countess did not speak and he went on in a brave voice:

"Oh, well! All good things have to come to an end and now I have to put my shoulder to the wheel, or whatever the saying is, and find work of some sort. It'll not be difficult. I know several firms who'll be glad to have me."

"And that means you will have to live in London?" the Dowager Countess asked.

"Not necessarily," Felix answered. "It might be Birmingham or Manchester, or any big Industrial town."

"Felix, you cannot leave me!"

It was the cry he had hoped to hear and he said with a well simulated throb in his voice:

"You can't think I wish to do so! You've given me so much happiness, Roseline, that I can never forget what we have meant to each other. But it must be good-bye!"

"No! Felix, no! I cannot let you go. How much money do you want?"

There was a desperation in the tone of her voice which he did not miss.

"I can't tell you," he said. "I'm ashamed that I've let things get to such a state."

"How much is it?" Roseline Kelvedon insisted.

"Eight thousand pounds!"

She gave a little gasp. Then she said:

"I will find it, you know I will find it, Felix. It will not be easy. I cannot take it out of the Estate money, for the accountants who check the accounts every month would be certain to report such a large sum to Roque."

"I wouldn't wish your son to know of this," Felix said quickly.

"He will not know," the Dowager Countess said confidently. "I will find the money myself. I think I have almost enough, and anyway I can always borrow on my jewellery."

"Yes, of course," Felix agreed, "but I can't allow you to do that."

He had forgotten the jewellery, he thought to himself.

The fabulous collection of jewels, some belonging personally to the Dowager Countess and some being Kelvedon heirlooms, was immensely valuable.

He wished now he had made the sum he had required ten thousand pounds. On jewels such as Roseline possessed she could raise any money she asked for, but he had not thought of it until this moment.

He cursed himself for a fool and then thought that if he could get the eight thousand now it might be worth waiting a few months before he left to collect a little more.

"I will write you a cheque on my private account," Roseline Kelvedon was saying. "Promise me, Felix darling, you will never get into such straits again. Give me your bills as they come in and I will settle them. When one has to find such a very large sum at a moment's notice it makes things difficult."

"You have only to smile at your bank manager," Felix said, "and he'll give you a million on loan without needing any further security. I know I would."

"Are you flattering me, darling?" the Dowager Countess asked. "It is something you have omitted to do for some time."

"It's only because I've been so worried."

"Why did you not tell me, you silly boy! Money is such a boring barrier to come between us and spoil our happiness."

"It's extremely boring if you haven't got any!" Felix said. "You ought to let me find some work, Roseline."

"I cannot do without you—you know that! You are mine and I will not share you with anyone else again!"

There was that hint of suspicion in her tone and Felix cursed himself for having been caught in the Duchesse's room. He had been certain that Roseline had gone out into the garden and that he would be free of her for at least half an hour.

But she had come creeping back, and now he knew that she would be even more watchful and suspicious of him than she had been before.

Granted he had been a fool to be nearly caught red-handed with her trainer's daughter at Newmarket.

She had been a pretty piece and not in the least reluctant to do whatever he wished. It was just unfortunate that Roseline Kelvedon should have come in search of him and found them together in one of the loose-boxes.

He had lied his way back into favour, but he had known that after that she had been more watchful and far more suspicious.

He told himself that never again would he become involved with a woman who was so much older than himself.

He really liked very young and unsophisticated girls. It gave him a sense of power and omnipotence. But the type of girl he fancied had no money, and this meant he was back where he came in, seeking the security of a rich wife.

"Come along to my room," Roseline Kelvedon said. "I will write you a cheque right away. I do not wish you to be worried or to act as strangely and unkindly as you have these past two days."

She smiled as she said:

"I know you so well, Felix darling. I was sure you had something on your mind."

"I was wondering how I could break it to you that I had to leave," Felix answered.

"That is something which is never going to happen," Roseline Kelvedon said. "It is so wonderful that we can be here together. I have never, and that is the truth, Felix, been so happy."

'It's more than I am!' he thought savagely.

But he put his arm round her shoulders as they went towards her Boudoir, which opened out of her bedroom at the far end of the corridor.

The room was filled with flowers, some from the vast hot-houses which occupied nearly an acre of land in the kitchen-gardens, and some from the borders running along the side of the great lawns which were a kaleidoscope of colour as the early summer flowers came into bloom.

There were comfortable sofas and chairs and the room was redolent with the exotic scent that Roseline Kelvedon always used and for which she sent to Paris.

She sat down at an exquisite French *secrétaire,* opened a drawer and took out her cheque book.

She wrote Felix's name on the cheque and filled in eight thousand pounds in her elegant, rather bold writing. Then she signed it and held it out to him.

"A present for someone I love," she smiled.

"Thank you, Roseline. You know how grateful I am."

He slipped the cheque into the inside pocket of his coat.

"How grateful are you?" Roseline Kelvedon asked softly.

She looked up at him, her red mouth curved invitingly, and he knew what was expected of him.

107

"Let me show you," he answered and pulled her into his arms.

* * * * * * *

Olinda finished the curtain in the Duchesse's room an hour after she had heard Felix Hanson and the Dowager Countess moving away and she knew that by a miracle she had been reprieved.

She then picked up her embroidery silks, wiped her scissors, which she saw with distaste had a touch of blood on their points, and went back to her own room.

She rang the bell and when Lucy appeared she said:

"Would you ask Mrs. Kingston if the cover from the Duchesse's bed can be brought here for me to work on it?"

"Yes, of course, Miss," Lucy replied.

Olinda was sure that Felix Hanson would tell the Dowager Countess that he had not been aware that she was in the bedroom, and she thought that if later Her Ladyship went to find out the truth for herself she would in fact find no one there.

It was just a question of timing: if she was found working in her own room it might substantiate his story and allay any suspicion the Dowager Countess might have.

She loathed with every tissue of her body being involved in his lies, but she knew that to be dismissed now, when there was so much work still for her to do, would be heartbreaking.

Besides she had to admit to herself that she could not bear to leave not knowing what the Earl would do or whether he would pay any attention to what she had suggested to him last night.

It was like reading a book and losing it half-way through so that one never knew the end of the story.

It was quite difficult to guess what the end of the Kelvedon drama would be.

Although she had told the Earl that he should stay at

108

home she wondered if any man feeling as he did about his mother's liaison could bear to be reminded of it day after day.

It would be a humiliation for him to have to be even distantly polite to Felix Hanson, and Olinda could understand the revulsion the mere sight of the man caused in him.

It was the same feeling she had herself for Felix Hanson—not that what she felt was of any account!

Yet what was the alternative for the Earl? To go back to Paris, and if what Mademoiselle le Bronc said was true, eat out his heart longing for his home, for his country, for his horses, for his possessions and everything that was a part of his blood?

"Why can his mother not understand what she is doing to him?" Olinda asked.

She had tried last night to make him see the Dowager Countess's point of view. Her looks were fading, she was growing old and everything she had valued most would wither and die together with her youth.

Olinda had wondered this morning when she awoke how she had been brave enough to speak as she had, to champion a woman who fundamentally was the opposite to everything she believed was good and noble.

Olinda knew that to her mother the Dowager Countess would be quite simply an evil woman.

Lady Selwyn was very strait-laced and she had often deprecated to Olinda the loose morals of what was known as 'The Marlborough Set'—the gay, pleasure-loving, fast society which surrounded the Prince of Wales.

"They are a bad example to the country as a whole," she had said to her daughter in her gentle voice, "and I cannot understand how the Prince of Wales can allow his name to be coupled with such women as Mrs. Langtry or the Countess of Warwick, who has proclaimed the Prince's infatuation so openly that it is gossiped about in the common newspapers!"

Olinda had not been particularly interested at the

time because she had known it was very unlikely she would ever come in contact with the social figures who shocked and distressed her mother.

But now there was a love-affair taking place in the house where she was working, and she could see all too clearly the repercussions it had not only upon the Earl but on all the household.

The servants disliked Mr. Hanson and resented his presence. Yet last night she had tried to find an explanation to the Earl for his mother's behaviour.

She thought now that he was right and there was in fact no excuse for the way in which the Dowager Countess had behaved, apparently even when he was still a boy.

Olinda had admired the Duchesse de Mazarin, in spite of her lack of morals: she had given the King not only her body but her mind, and had inspired him in a way no other woman had been able to do before.

Her scintillating and brilliant brain had been as important to him as the beauty of her body.

Olinda remembered reading that in the Salon Hortense de Mazarin had set up in London, her knowledge of philosophy, her exchange of witticisms with the greatest brains of the age and the brilliant cut and thrust of debate had brought the King a new interest and an intellectual pleasure that he had missed ever since his return to England.

That was love on a very different plane, Olinda told herself, from the Dowager Countess's passion for a man over twenty years her junior and her inferior in both breeding and intellect.

She felt herself shudder as she thought about Felix Hanson.

She longed to comfort the Earl and sweep away his bitterness; to try to persuade him that his mother's behaviour must not be allowed to poison his life.

There was so much lying before him, so much for him to do; he must not be handicapped by a woman who had never considered her son or cared enough to deny herself a sensuous pleasure.

As Olinda sewed away at the cover the housemaids brought her and laid out on the table in her room, she found it impossible to think of anything but the problems around her.

The fantasies which had so often occupied her mind in the past had all now become concentrated in the real-life story of the Earl.

Lucy came at luncheon time to move Olinda's work from the table. As she brought out the white linen cloth she said:

"*M'mselle* has left this morning."

"Has she?" Olinda asked in surprise.

"His Lordship took her to Derby Station," Lucy replied, "and she told Mrs. Kingston before she left that she was longing to get back to Paris. 'All the same, *M'mselle*, I hope you've had a nice rest,' Mrs. Kingston said politely.

"'I'll be resting a long time in the grave,' M'mselle answered her. 'This place is like a crypt and I don't know how you stand it!'"

Lucy laughed.

"What do you think of that, Miss! A crypt indeed! Mrs. Kingston was really shocked, and when she told Mr. Burrows he said, 'You never know what these foreigners will say next, there're not like us and a good thing too, if you ask me!'"

Olinda laughed, she could not help herself. She could almost hear the old butler saying it.

At the same time her heart was singing with joy! The Earl had not gone back to France with Mademoiselle le Bronc!

Perhaps that meant he intended to stay at home permanently, and she only wished that she could see him and that he would tell her of his intentions.

Then she told herself it was very unlikely that he would want to speak to her again.

Last night, because he had been so desperate, he had turned to her because she was a stranger and because, as he had said to her on the island, she had not seemed real but part of a dream.

It had all been part of the starlight, the stillness of the air, the exquisite view down the lake, and the great house silhouetted against the sky.

Nothing could have been common-place in such a setting, and so they had talked as Olinda had never talked to a man before, and the Earl had confided in her because she was a stranger.

Were they to meet again in the day-time, Olinda thought, the Earl might feel embarrassed because he had spoken so frankly and they had discussed his mother as she was quite certain he had never discussed her with anyone else.

'Now he will avoid me,' she thought with a sigh, 'as I must avoid him.'

It was a depressing idea and she knew, as the day passed while she sat stitching away at the cover from the Duchesse's bed, she longed with an intensity that was almost physical to be with the Earl again and to talk to him.

Because she was sure what his feelings were, she knew that the one place she must not go when she had finished supper was to the Greek Temple on the island.

Resolutely she let herself out of the same door as she had done the night before, but now she walked deliberately through the gardens which lay at the back of the house.

The sun was still bright although the shadows were growing longer, and the Earl, Olinda knew, would be at dinner.

There would be no one to see her wend her way through the rose-gardens with an ageing sundial in the centre of them, and pass again through yew hedges.

She found the gardens as they sloped upwards were laid out in a manner which was a continual surprise and delight to anyone walking in them.

She found a bowling-alley and what she knew was a maze, and child-like she longed to explore but was too frightened of getting lost.

She found a small cascade falling down into a water-garden that was bright with small shrubs and exotic plants which she knew must have been brought from many parts of the world.

She climbed up the side of the cascade by a small flight of steps and finally left the gardens for a shrubbery brilliant with rhododendrons, crimson, white and purple.

Their colours seemed to flare like flames against the darkness of the pine trees behind them.

The path twisted and turned until finally Olinda found herself at the top of a hill with Kelvedon down below her.

There was a statue of a goddess, beautifully sculptured in white marble, and there was a seat beneath it on which she could sit and look down into the valley below.

She could see the gardens, the great house, and beyond it the lake.

Through the branches of the trees she could catch a glimpse of the Greek Temple and she wondered if perhaps the Earl would go there and expect to find her waiting for him.

Then she laughed at her presumption.

He could have no interest in her personally! She had just been a face speaking in the darkness, and because he had been so desperate her words had seemed important and he had given her an attention which he would never have accorded her at any other time.

How could she expect anything else when she was nothing but an employee in his house?

The view was very beautiful. The sun had begun to sink, filling the sky with colour, and there was only the sounds from the woods around to disturb the peace of the passing day.

There was the flutter of birds coming in to roost and the rustle of small animals moving in the undergrowth.

Olinda wondered how many people had come to this

spot to find peace and perhaps escape from the difficulties and problems that awaited them in the house below.

Kelvedon was built for happiness as she had told the Earl last night.

She reflected how people tore themselves in pieces with the passion and violence of their emotions, and yet it was such a waste of time.

In reality they had so few years to live, and while they died Kelvedon remained, strong and impregnable.

She was thinking of all the Kelvedons who had lived there and particularly of the present Earl. She felt she could see his face as vividly as if he was beside her and hear his voice with all its varying intonations as when he had spoken to her last night.

Then suddenly again her dreams became reality!

"I knew this was where I would find you," a deep voice said.

The Earl sat down beside her on the seat.

She did not start, she only knew it seemed inevitable that he should appear because she had been thinking of him.

"How did you know I would be . . here?" she asked.

"I was sure that you would feel too shy to go to the Temple," he replied, "and this is the other place where I come to dream and to find peace."

"I did not . . know that."

"Perhaps not consciously," he said, "but undoubtedly unconsciously. You see, we cannot avoid each other, you and I. As I anticipated, you are here."

She glanced at him and thought that he looked younger and happier than she had expected.

He was in evening clothes and she wondered vaguely how he could have escaped so quickly from the Dining room and a dinner of many courses.

Then she realised she must have been sitting below the statue for quite a long time, because now the sun had gone behind the trees and the sky was deepening in the East.

"Are you not interested enough to want a report?" the Earl asked.

"A report?" Olinda echoed in surprise.

"On how I have carried out your commands."

He was laughing at her, Olinda thought, but it was not unkind. In fact there was an intimacy about his tone that made her feel a little shy.

"I hoped you would be interested," he went on.

"I am interested in anything you have to tell me," Olinda answered, "but I thought that perhaps today . ."

He smiled and it seemed to transform his face.

"I knew exactly what you would be thinking," he said, "but you are quite wrong. I did not regret confiding in you. I do not feel embarrassed because we were frank with each other. I just wanted to find out if you had been right, and you were."

Olinda looked at him in astonishment.

"How could he have known," she asked herself, "what has been in my mind all day?"

Then knowing what he wanted her to say, she asked: "Will you tell me what you have done?"

"After my guest left to return to France—and as you would have told me if you had been brave enough, I made a mistake in bringing her here—I have been visiting my farms."

"They were pleased to see you?" Olinda asked.

"They certainly seemed to be!" he replied. "I do not think I understood before that those who live on a great Estate feel that they own the proprietor just as he owns them."

"You are a part of their lives."

"A very large part," the Earl agreed, "but I did not realise it."

"And now?"

"They want me to be here," he said. "They want to be able to explain to me what they are doing, show me their achievements, ask my help when things go wrong."

"And that has made you happy?"

"Everyone wishes to be wanted. I suppose my father would have told me, if I had listened, how interwoven one is with the lives of people who work on one's land, who give you by their labours their very life."

Olinda clasped her hands together.

"I am glad . . so very glad . . that you have found that out for . . yourself."

"I should have known it before," the Earl said. "Now I must try to make up lost time. I have wasted two years and I must somehow redeem them."

"I know you will be able to do so," Olinda said in a low voice.

"How can you know that?"

"I know it in the . . same way as I knew last night what I must . . tell you to . . do."

The Earl was silent. Then he said:

"Tell me about yourself."

"There is nothing to tell," Olinda said quickly. "My mother is ill and I need money for her food and medicines. I have very few talents but I can embroider."

"I should have said you had many talents," the Earl said, "and perhaps perception, clairvoyance or call it what you will, is one of them."

"Perhaps instinct would be a better word," Olinda said quietly.

"An instinct for what is right. Could any human being ask for more?"

The Earl looked at Olinda as he spoke, seeing her hair very fair against the darkness of the trees that surrounded them.

"Do you know what this goddess represents?" he asked.

"I am afraid I forgot to look," Olinda replied. "I was so entranced by the view.

"She is Athene, the Goddess of Wisdom," the Earl explained, "who knew more things than all the Gods and men put together. Is not wisdom one of the things that you thought important to love?"

"Very important," Olinda said gravely, thinking of Hortense de Mazarin.

"And wisdom is what few women have," the Earl went on. "Yet it is what most men are afraid to find in a pretty woman."

"Afraid?" Olinda questioned.

"No man wants a woman who is cleverer than he is himself."

"I think we are talking about two different things," Olinda said slowly. "Cleverness in a way can be frightening, but wisdom is something quite different."

"You are right, of course you are right!" the Earl said. "What is it about you, Olinda, that you can always put things into the right perspective? The instinct of wisdom! Yes, that indeed is what a man needs!"

Unexpectedly he rose to his feet.

"Come," he said, "I will take you home. When it gets dark it is hard to find the path back through the wood."

Olinda wondered if he was making an excuse to be rid of her, but when they entered the wood she found that, as he had said, it was quite difficult even in the twilight to find the way.

There were also the steps down the side of the cascade to be negotiated, and by the time they reached the gardens the light had almost gone and the dusk was closing in.

They walked in silence across the velvet lawns and yet it seemed to Olinda that somehow they were speaking to each other.

She was not certain what they said, she only knew she was glad, with a strange gladness she could not explain to herself to be beside the Earl and know that he was there.

"It is because he is doing what I advised," she told herself.

But she knew that was not really the answer.

They reached the side-door to which Olinda had the key. He took it from her, turned the key in the lock and held it out to her.

"Good night, Olinda," he said, "and thank you."

She took the key from him and as she did so her

fingers touched his. She felt something like a shock run through her body.

She looked up at him inquiringly and he bent his head as if to kiss her cheek.

"Thank you," he began to say—but his lips found hers.

Again there was that sense of shock, and now it was like a streak of lightning running through her.

His arms were round her and his mouth took possession of hers.

For a moment it was a warmth and excitement, a feeling she had never known and somehow just as she had expected a kiss to be.

Then suddenly it was a wonder, a rapture, something so exquisite, so perfect that it was beyond thought and expression.

She felt as if a vivid and blinding light encompassed them, and they were no longer two people but part of the wonder of Heaven itself.

"This is Divine!" Olinda thought, "and we are no longer human but gods!"

Then the ecstasy she felt made it impossible to think. It was so supreme, a rapture so unbelievable that time stood still. . . .

She did not realise she had moved, but she found herself inside the house.

The door closed behind her and she was alone.

* * * * * * *

Olinda lay for a long time face downwards on her bed. She had not undressed and she could not remember how she had found her way up the stairs and into her own room.

Her whole body was pulsating, vibrating as if to the music of angels.

She could not bear to come back to earth to face the common-place to know that the light was gone and the glory she had felt had gone with it.

"Why did I not realise," she asked herself, "that love is like that?"

Why she had not known from the moment she met the Earl and saw him standing in the window, that he was the man who could evoke in her the rapture which she had read about, and searched for, but had no idea how to find it?

This was the Holy Grail of which she had spoken. This was love as it was meant to be, the complete love of body, mind and soul.

Then, as if she fell down from a great height into a valley of darkness, she told herself that, while she might feel like that, the Earl would feel very differently.

He must have kissed hundreds of women and she had been just one more.

He had been elated with his success during the day, and grateful to her because she had suggested to him what he should do!

That was all! There had been no talk of love between them tonight. He was not in love with her nor ever likely to be.

She had nothing to offer the Earl of Kelvedon, who was a matrimonial catch in the social world, and who must have been pursued for his title and his great possessions ever since he had grown up.

That he had been obsessed by his unhappiness over his mother and his hatred of her paramour did not alter the fact that socially he was very eligible and was also a most attractive man.

"How could I think that for one moment he might be interested in me?" Olinda asked herself. "Even if he knew who I was, it would make no difference. I have nothing to offer him, nothing!"

With that thought the last remnant of the glory that had swept her up into a heaven of happiness ebbed away to leave her in a very special hell.

'If I had never felt like that, even for a moment, I should not have missed it,' she thought.

She knew now that never again would life seem quite the same.

Perhaps that was overdramatic, perhaps she was exaggerating what had happened. Yet she knew that, having touched the Divine for one fleeting second, she could never again accept a substitute.

"I have always known it was like that," she told herself.

But she also thought that in allowing the Earl to kiss her she had in fact destroyed any chance she might ever have of happiness.

"How could I have known? How could I have guessed what he meant to do?" she asked miserably.

She told herself that he would think of her as Felix Hanson had, as a woman of no principles, willing to flirt with any man who paid her attention.

Perhaps he would even believe she was willing to let a flirtation go further and become a love affair.

She was appalled at the thought.

"Could he think that? How could he?"

Yet she knew it was very possible.

Girls who were properly brought up as she had been did not allow a man they had met on no more than three occasions to kiss them passionately.

She had neither struggled nor protested, but had surrendered herself to a rapture that had swept away thought itself.

Perhaps being kissed is like that for everybody, Olinda wondered, and knew the answer.

If Felix Hanson had kissed her it would have been very different. Then she would have felt disgusted, revolted, affronted.

It was only the Earl who could awake in her sensations which until then she did not know existed.

"How could I have let him? Why did I not anticipate that that might happen?"

She asked herself the same question over and over again. Then because there was no answer she allowed herself almost reluctantly and because she could not help it to live again the rapture and the inexpressible wonder of his lips.

"I have talked about love and I have thought about it," Olinda told herself, "but I did not know at all what it

120

was like. Now I can understand why Kings have given up their thrones, why men have started wars and others have died a thousand deaths to prove their love!"

She drew in her breath.

"It is greater, more marvellous, more overwhelming than any human being can conceive. It is in truth Divine."

Then because she thought she would never find it again and the marvel of it was lost to her forever, she began to cry.

Tears of self-pity ran down her cheeks and she knew that no amount of wise common-sense could wipe them away.

CHAPTER SIX

Felix Hanson came down the stairs whistling.

He was feeling in exceptionally good temper, because he had beaten the professional who had come from Derby to play tennis with him.

This was the first time he had done so, after many strenuous battles.

He was also happy because he knew that on Monday morning the Dowager Countess's cheque for eight thousand pounds would pass into his bank account and he could then begin to plan how he could return to London.

He had spent most of the night contemplating his assets and thinking that once his outstanding bills were settled he would be in a comparatively sound financial position.

There should be well over two thousand pounds left over from the cheque, on top of which he had quite a number of expensive presents the Dowager Countess had given him.

They included cuff-links, tie-pins, a gold watch and chain, a signet-ring, and various other items of jewellery, all of which were cashable should the necessity arise.

He had also three race-horses that were registered under his name, and although he intended to try to sell them he felt it might be difficult to do so as they were in the Kelvedon stables.

He was well aware how bitter and vindictive Roseline Kelvedon would be when she finally realised he intended to leave her and was in fact no longer interested in her as a woman.

There was, however, Felix told himself, little she could do except to be spiteful.

She would try to prevent him from claiming his race-horses, his car and any other gifts over which there might be disputed ownership.

At the same time his prospects and the future looked

fair, and as he reached the Hall and glanced at the large grandfather-clock standing against one wall he realised that he had dressed early and there was another twenty minutes before dinner would be announced.

As he walked towards the Library he saw that the footman on duty was Henry, a young man who had an obsession for cars and whom Felix Hanson had found useful on several occasions.

"Good-evening, Henry," he said.

"Good-evening, Sir," Henry replied respectfully.

"Is Her Ladyship downstairs yet?"

"No, Sir. I understand Her Ladyship had a headache and has been resting. But Mr. Burrows believes she will be coming down to dinner."

Felix Hanson smiled to himself.

'That lets me off the hook,' he thought. 'Roseline will go to bed early and I'll have a chance of seeing "little grey eyes".'

"There is something you can do for me, Henry," he said in a low voice. "If I give you a note, will you slip it under Miss Selwyn's door as you did the other one I gave you?"

"Of course, Sir."

"Then I will have it ready in a couple of minutes," Felix Hanson said.

He hurried into the Library and sat down at the desk.

He pulled a piece of writing-paper onto the blotter and wrote:

"I have to see you and it's very urgent! I'll come to your Sitting-Room at about ten o'clock. Leave the door unlocked."

He folded the writing-paper, went to the door of the Library and signalled to Henry who was waiting in the Hall.

He put the note in the footman's hand and walked across the room to stand looking into the garden, whistling softly to himself.

He had no intention of leaving Kelvedon before he had kissed the pretty embroiderer. He had promised himself that pleasure and he had no intention of forgoing it.

The Library door was flung open suddenly and he turned round to face the Dowager Countess. A glance at her face was enough to tell him that she was in one of her rages.

She walked into the centre of the room. Then she said, her voice low and yet the mere fact that she was controlling it making it sound more ominous:

"How dare you! How dare you intrigue with a woman in my house behind my back!"

Felix Hanson walked slowly towards her.

"I have no idea what you are talking about, Roseline."

"You know perfectly well what I am saying," the Dowager Countess said, "and do not bother to lie. I have just taken this from the footman who was carrying it upstairs."

She held out his note as she spoke.

As Felix Hanson stared at it wondering what he should say, the Dowager Countess continued:

"The flunkey will be sacked just as I am sacking you. You can get out of my house and I never want to see you again!"

"Now, Roseline," Felix Hanson said soothingly, "this is ridiculous!"

"I warned you the last time," the Dowager Countess said her voice rising. "I warned you then that I would not stand for your philandering or seducing other women while you belong to me. Well, you have made your choice. Now you can get out!"

"You're being ridiculous," Felix Hanson expostulated. "You know I love you. As a matter of fact I wanted to speak to the girl about making you a present for your birthday."

"You lie! You lie!" the Dowager Countess shrieked. "I was a fool ever to have believed in you—ever to have thought you cared for anything but my money and what you can get out of me."

She paused to draw in her breath and her green eyes were blazing as she went on:

"Money is what you have been after, and now you are going to be disappointed in that, if in nothing else. I will stop the cheque I gave you. It will not be presented until Monday and I can assure you that from this moment it is not worth the paper it is written on!"

She waited, and as he did not speak, she went on:

"When you go, leave behind all the presents I have given you, otherwise I will sue you for them!"

"You have entirely the wrong idea!" Felix Hanson said feebly. "Let me explain . ."

"There is nothing you can say that I am willing to hear," the Dowager Countess raged. "I have listened to you for too long. You have deceived me over and over again, but I was such a fool I did not realise it! Now get out of my house before I have you thrown out!"

She walked across the room as she spoke. She pulled open the Library door and turned round to say:

"I do not want to hear from you or see you again—ever! Is that clear?"

Her voice rang out and she walked across the Hall towards the Salon, her whole body trembling with fury.

She had only just reached it when from the opposite direction down the broad corridor the Earl appeared, moving so swiftly that he seemed almost to be running.

"Mama!" he exclaimed. "I wish to speak with you."

"What about?" the Dowager Countess asked.

She walked into the Salon trying to get her breath, determined that for the moment her son should not know what had upset her.

She knew it would give him pleasure to learn that she had finished with Felix Hanson, and she had no wish to give anyone pleasure. She hated all men, even her own son!

The Earl followed her into the Salon to say furiously:

"What the devil do you think you have been doing to the Chapel?"

"The Chapel?" the Dowager Countess repeated blankly. For the moment she could not force herself to comprehend what he was saying.

"Yes, to the Chapel," the Earl said. "That perfect example of 17th century architecture which has hardly been touched since its completion in 1680. I say 'hardly'—because God knows what you have done to it now!"

"Oh, of course. I remember," the Dowager Countess replied. "Felix wanted to use it as a gymnasium, and as it had the best light and was in fact exactly the right shape, he assured me the equipment would not damage the murals."

"Have you no respect—no reverence for anything?" the Earl demanded, and she realised how angry he was.

"After all, the Chapel was never used," she replied defensively.

"And whose fault was that?" the Earl enquired. "It was used when my father was alive, and my grandfather, and my ancestors before them. But a House of God was never intended to be a gymnasium for some pimp who took your fancy!"

The Dowager Countess did not speak, and after a moment he said:

"Can you really care so little for Kelvedon? Can it mean so little to you that you would deface and destroy one of the most perfect parts of the house?"

He spoke with a bitterness which vibrated through him, and his words seemed to sweep away the last vestige of his mother's self-control.

"Kelvedon! Kelvedon! Always Kelvedon!" she screamed. "Nothing counts for you, for your father or for anyone else except this house! This monstrous museum full of souvenirs of dead people!"

She paused, and because she had been hurt by Felix Hanson she was determined to hurt her son.

"I have had enough of Kelvedon!" she raged. "I will tell you what I am going to do. I am going to close the house! I am going to sack all those doddering old servants you insist upon retaining! I am going to live in London or abroad, and I'll spend every penny on which I can lay my hands in enjoying myself!"

She moved towards the door.

"They can start putting up the shutters to-morrow!"

"Mama, you cannot mean that!" the Earl exclaimed.

"I mean it!" the Countess answered. "I mean every word of it!"

She walked across the Hall as she spoke and started to climb the stairs.

The Earl followed her.

"Mama, let us talk this over sensibly."

For a moment the Countess did not answer him but continued up the stairs.

"Mama!" the Earl said pleadingly.

She turned her head to look over the banister.

"I mean exactly what I say," she answered. "This house will be closed and the servants dismissed. If you want to keep it going, you can of course sell the pictures off the walls, one by one!"

There was a vindictive spite in her voice that was unmistakable.

For a moment the Earl glared at her. Then he replied furiously:

"I will see you dead first!"

Neither mother nor son moved.

Then with an insolent laugh the Dowager Countess continued up the stairs and the Earl with a muttered oath rushed out of the front door and down the steps.

Old Burrows, who had come into the Hall to announce dinner, stood staring after him with consternation on his face.

It was ten minutes later that Lucy carried to Olinda the news of what had occurred.

"There's been a terrible row, Miss," she said as she carried the first course into Olinda's Sitting-Room and set the tray down on a side-table.

"A row?" Olinda enquired quickly.

"And over you, Miss, so I understand."

Olinda's eyes were very large and apprehensive as she asked:

"Did you . . say it was over . . me, Lucy?"

"Yes, indeed, Miss. Mr. Hanson gave Henry a note to

slip under your door, as he had told him to slip one there the first night you arrived."

Olinda drew in her breath.

So it had not been Felix Hanson who had come to her locked door as she had thought, but one of the footmen.

Somehow it seemed even more degrading that he should involve the servants in his intrigues.

"Mr. Hanson wrote you another note to-night," Lucy said, "and he asked Henry to bring it up to you. But Henry's so stupid! I suppose really he's not been here long enough to know his job."

"What happened?" Olinda asked faintly.

"He comes up the front stairs, if you can imagine such a thing, Miss. If Mr. Burrows had caught him he'd have been in trouble all right, but as it was he meets Her Ladyship."

"Her Ladyship?" Olinda repeated.

"Yes, Miss. She takes the note from him and when she reads it she goes white as a sheet, so Henry says."

Olinda sat at the table as if turned to stone.

This meant, she thought, that she would be dismissed immediately, and she knew it was not only the money she would no longer earn for her mother that she minded, but also that she would have to leave the Earl.

"What .. happened?" she asked.

"Her Ladyship goes into the Library to find Mr. Hanson," Lucy said, "and would you believe, Miss, she tells him he's to get out of the house and she never wants to see him again!"

"How do you know this?"

"Well, Henry was trying to listen to what was being said. Then when she opens the door she tells Mr. Hanson clear as clear that she never wants to hear from him or see him again!"

"How could he have .. written to .. me?" Olinda asked beneath her breath.

"That's not all, Miss."

"What else?" Olinda asked, feeling that nothing worse could happen.

"Her Ladyship goes into the Salon and His Lordship comes from the Chapel in a terrible rage!"

"The Chapel?" Olinda exclaimed.

"Yes, Miss. He had Mr. Lanceworth along there at about 6 o'clock and you could hear his anger all down the corridors."

"But why? Why the Chapel?" Olinda enquired.

"Mr. Hanson had it turned into a gymnasium, Miss, and His Lordship didn't like it."

"I am not surprised."

"Anyway," Lucy continued with relish, "he comes straight to speak about it to Her Ladyship and he'd have been late for dinner as he wasn't changed."

Olinda made no comment as Lucy went on:

"They were shouting at each other in the Salon. Then Her Ladyship comes out and says that she's going to close the house and dismiss all the staff. His Lordship tries to plead with her, but she says that if he wants to keep the house open he can sell the pictures one by one."

Lucy paused dramatically before she finished:

"And His Lordship says: 'I'll see you dead first!'"

Olinda rose from the table to walk across the room to the window.

She found it hard to believe this had really happened— hard to credit that the Dowager Countess should have made such an appalling decision!

How could she, just at this moment when the Earl had decided to stay at home and take his rightful place in the County?

"Your dinner's getting cold, Miss," Lucy said from behind her.

"I do not want anything to eat, thank you, Lucy."

"Oh, Miss, Chef'll be ever so upset!" Lucy replied. "His Lordship's stalked out of the house and it doesn't look as if he'll come back for dinner. Her Ladyship's locked herself in her bed-room and won't even let in Miss Heyman, her lady's-maid."

Lucy picked up the dish to carry it back to the side-table.

"That just leaves Mr. Hanson in the Dining-Room," she said, "I bet he's eating his head off and enjoying it, although it's all his fault!"

Yes, it was all Felix Hanson's fault, Olinda thought to herself.

How could he have written a note to her which the Dowager Countess could intercept?

She had no idea what was in the note, but she guessed he was trying to arrange for her to meet him as he had done before.

"It is all his fault," she repeated and thought of the Earl.

She knew exactly where he would have gone, where he would be trying to find some sort of peace in his despair.

She was aware what a blow this would be to him.

That his mother should close Kelvedon would inflict a mortal wound on her son! Even while he had exiled himself from his home, he had thought of it, dreamt of it and imagined it as it always had been.

"Are you sure there's nothing more I can get you, Miss?" Lucy asked. "There's a nice dish of guinea-fowl here. You'd enjoy it—you would really!"

"I am sorry, Lucy," Olinda said. "I am rather upset by what you have told me and I would like to be alone."

"I understand, Miss. We're all upset, if it comes to that!"

Lucy paused to say:

"I suppose I'll get another job, but Mr. Burrows was saying he's too old, and Mr. Higman—that's His Lordship's valet—was so happy he was not to be retired that he seemed like a young man again. I suppose now he'll be in tears."

Olinda did not answer and Lucy went from the room.

For some minutes Olinda sat looking out of the window with unseeing eyes. Then she knew what she must do.

She opened the door of her Sitting-Room and found, as she had expected, that the passage was empty.

Lucy would have gone downstairs, and she could

imagine all too vividly the consternation being felt by the staff.

She slipped down the back staircase and let herself out through the garden-door.

Keeping to the shrubbery so that she was out of sight of anyone looking through the windows, she found her way through the yew-hedges and the walled garden and orchard towards the lake.

The Greek Temple was gleaming white against the brilliance of the setting sun.

It was earlier in the day than when Olinda had been there before, and she thought as she crossed the Chinese bridge that it was even lovelier than it had been at dusk.

Now she could see the golden kingcups lining the banks of the lake, the swans like graceful galleons reflected in its smooth surface, and a profusion of red damask roses climbing over the sides of the balustrade.

As she had expected, the Earl was there.

He was sitting on the seat bending forward, his head in his hands.

She stood looking at him and he knew without looking up that she had come.

"I have failed, Olinda!" he said.

At the sound of his voice she moved forward to sit down beside him.

"No! No!" Olinda asserted. "This is not your fault—you must not blame yourself."

"I should not have raged at her," he said, "but I could not bear to find that the Chapel had been desecrated in such a way—the place where my father lay when he was dead, where I was Christened, a place which has been a part of my life and that of my ancestors all down the centuries."

"I understand," Olinda said softly.

"I was angry—so very angry!" the Earl said, almost like a child confessing a sin to someone in authority.

"Your mother was already upset by something else before you spoke to her," Olinda said. "I think perhaps she may change her mind."

The Earl drew in his breath and sat back against the seat.

He did not look at Olinda, but at the lake lying in front of him and at the great house in the distance.

"Why should you think that?"

"She had just dismissed Mr. Hanson," Olinda explained in a low voice.

"Dismissed him?" the Earl exclaimed, his voice ringing out like a pistol-shot. "How do you know? And why should she have done that?"

"Because he wrote a note to me which your mother intercepted," Olinda replied very quietly.

Now the Earl turned to look at her with an incredulous expression on his face.

"He wrote a note to you?" he repeated.

"It is the second time he has done so," Olinda explained. "There was a note pushed under my door the first night I arrived to say that he was waiting to see me in the Library at midnight."

"What did you do about it?"

"I tore it into a thousand pieces!" Olinda answered. "But I . . I was . . afraid of him!"

The Earl's lips tightened.

"Because I know it would upset you," he said after a moment. "I will not express what I feel about that unutterable cad."

"I think he feels he is irresistible to women, and no-one in my position could refuse to do as he wished," Olinda murmured.

"Nothing you could say about him could make me loathe him any more than I do already!" the Earl said.

"Anyway, your mother, having taken the note from the footman who was to bring it upstairs to me, read it, then she apparently told Mr. Hanson she had finished with him."

The Earl did not speak. Then after a moment Olinda went on:

"Can you not understand? She had been deeply hurt and so she wanted to hurt you. I think to-morrow, when

132

Mr. Hanson has gone, you will be able to make her change her mind."

"I doubt it," the Earl said. "Even if she is well rid of him, there will be other men. There have always been other men! And I think she hates Kelvedon!"

"That is in a way understandable," Olinda said. "It means so much to you, and I expect it meant so much to your father that she is jealous of it."

"Would every woman be jealous of it?" the Earl enquired.

"I do not think so, unless they wished to focus your entire attention upon themselves," Olinda said. "But your mother is so beautiful that I feel she could never countenance a rival."

"I understand," the Earl replied, "but whatever you may say to try to comfort me, Olinda, I have a feeling we have reached the parting of the ways. My mother will go to London, taking all the money with her."

He was silent for a moment. Then he said with a pain in his voice that was unbearable:

"How can I let the people who trust me suffer? Burrows, who is too old to find another job; Higman, whom I have kept on although he is past retiring age; Mrs. Kingston, who has never known any other home and who feels the same way about Kelvedon as I do?"

"I know," Olinda said softly, "and that is why you must find a solution."

"A solution?" the Earl exclaimed. "And how do you think I can find that?"

"You have to think of one," Olinda said. "You have to!"

The insistence in her voice made him look at her for a moment in surprise. Then he said in a different tone:

"You are right! That is what I have to do!"

"Have you no money of your own?" Olinda enquired.

"I have about seven thousand a year," he answered. "Enough to be extremely comfortable as a bachelor travelling abroad, or living at the family house in London which, like everything else, is kept up by my mother."

He paused before he added bitterly:

"It would pay the expenses of Kelvedon for about a month, if one was economical."

"You have to save it," Olinda said. "Is there nothing you could sell?"

"I have no intention of accepting my mother's suggestion that I should sell the pictures from the walls," the Earl said and his voice was hard. "I have never thought they belonged to me personally, but to my son and the Kelvedons who will come after him. The Estate is the same. Every acre is a precious heritage which belongs to the future generations."

"And there is nothing else?" Olinda asked.

"There is a Hunting-Lodge in Leicestershire with a few hundred acres, and the racing stables at Newmarket," the Earl answered. "I suppose I could dispose of them. It would help to maintain Kelvedon for a little while. But let us face facts, Olinda: my mother is not an old woman. She may live for another twenty-five or thirty years."

"I cannot believe that sooner or later you could not make her see reason," Olinda said.

They both knew what they were thinking without putting it into words.

When the Dowager Countess's beauty had faded completely she would perhaps be glad to rely on her son, to acknowledge that he was the only man left in her life.

They talked, argued and discussed ways and means until the sun sank and the dusk faded into night.

Once again the stars were shining overhead and the moonlight touched the cupolas on the house and the top of the Grecian Temple.

The moon was stronger than the night before and Olinda could see the Earl's face quite clearly.

He talked to her with complete and utter frankness, asking her advice, listening to what she had to say, and gradually as the hours passed becoming more confident, more sure of himself.

"You can do it! I know you can do it!" she said. "It will be difficult. You must take everyone, the staff, the farmers, the whole Estate, into your confidence and ask them to work with you."

"Do you think they will agree?"

"I know they will agree. They love you and they trust you."

He drew a deep breath and it seemed to Olinda that he had thrown off his despair. There was a light of battle in his eyes which had not been there before.

"This is a challenge" she said softly. "If you accept it, I know that in the end you will sweep aside all the difficulties, all the problems, and win!"

There was a note of elation in her voice, and for the first time for hours he turned to look at her and saw the moonlight reflected in her eyes and shining on her hair.

"Why do you believe in me?" he asked.

"I just do," she replied simply.

"With all your heart?"

"With all my heart," she replied and knew it was the truth.

She had been so intent on thinking of him that not for one moment since she had come to the lake had she thought of herself.

All through the day she had been beset by doubts and despair and a kind of gnawing misery because of what had happened the previous night.

But now all she could think of was the difference she had made in him and that she had relieved his unhappiness and made him believe in himself.

For the first time she felt a little shy.

"It must be very .. late," she said. "I must go .. back."

She rose as she spoke and he too rose to his feet.

They stood looking at each other. Then the Earl said very quietly:

"You are going to help me, Olinda? I cannot do it without you."

"Are you .. sure you want .. me?"

He smiled.

"More sure than I have been of anything in my whole life."

"Then I will . . do whatever you . . want."

He put his arms around her and drew her close and she quivered at his touch, but he did not kiss her.

Instead he held her very tightly, his cheek against hers.

"I still do not believe you are real," he said. "You are my dream, the dream I have always dreamt here by the Temple. That is what I want you to be, because it is the only thing that will keep me sane and keep me fighting."

Olinda did not reply.

She only knew it was a happiness she had never imagined simply to be close to him, to feel his face against hers, to know that he needed her.

Then he released her.

"Go home, my darling," he said. "You will be tired to-morrow. I thought of you working so hard all day."

"What will you do?" Olinda enquired.

"I will sit here for a little while," he answered, "and think not only about Kelvedon, but also about you. Then I shall go for a walk. Perhaps up through the woods to the Goddess of Wisdom. I feel you and I, Olinda, are going to need her help in what lies ahead."

"She has watched over Kelvedon all these years," Olinda said. "I am sure she will not fail you now."

"You always say exactly the right thing."

The Earl took Olinda's hand and raised it to his lips.

"Thank you, my sweet," he said. "Those are inadequate words, but between us there is no need for them."

"Good-night," Olinda said softly.

She turned and walked away and without looking back crossed the Chinese bridge and found the path which led through the garden back to the house.

She felt strangely at peace with herself and knew she had left the same feeling of peace with the Earl.

It was as if they had both fought a tremendous battle side by side—a battle that had involved not only their hearts but also their minds and souls, and they had won!

Although there would be many battles in the future it was, Olinda thought, the most important.

She had reached the lawns in front of the house and

turned to seek the protection of the shrubs so that she could approach the garden-door unseen.

As she did so, she looked up at the great building, fairy-like in the light from the moon and knew it was worth fighting for.

Then she stiffened in sudden surprise.

* * * * * * *

When Olinda had finished her breakfast, Lucy cleared the table and put back on it the cover from the Countess's bed.

The maid was looking tired and had little to say this morning.

Olinda thought it was because she had doubtless stayed up late last night talking with the other servants and had perhaps been unable to sleep once she had gone to bed.

She herself also had slept very little.

While she behaved in a normal fashion, getting out her silks, setting them on the table ready to continue her work on the coverlet, she knew that a part of her was tense.

She was, in fact, waiting for the moment to receive her dismissal and go upstairs to pack her box.

It was unlikely that the Dowager Countess would let her off scot-free; for she would not for one moment believe that she had not welcomed Felix Hanson's advances.

Olinda wondered if he had already left the house. But she would not question Lucy, and for once the maid seemed to have nothing to chatter about.

It was half-past eight when Olinda started to work, and she had been stitching at the small, beautiful flowers on the coverlet for nearly an hour before she heard the sound of voices in the passage.

They seemed to be talking unusually loudly. Suddenly the door was thrown open and Lucy came rushing in.

"Oh, Miss! Miss!" she cried with an expression on her face which made Olinda stare at her with startled eyes.

"What is it, Lucy?"

137

"Her Ladyship, Miss! Oh, Miss, it's horrible!"

"What are you talking about, Lucy?"

"Her Ladyship's dead, Miss! They say that His Lordship killed her!"

For a moment Olinda was unable to move. Then she said sharply:

"That is ridiculous! Who is saying such things?"

"Everyone, Miss. When Miss Heyman called Her Ladyship a little while ago she found her—dead on the floor she was! She must have lain there all night! And they're accusing His Lordship!"

"How can they do such a thing?"

"He said it himself! His Lordship said: 'I'll see you dead first!' They all heard him—Mr. Burrows—Henry—James! They heard him say it, Miss!"

"He could never have done such a thing!" Olinda said angrily.

"They've sent for the Chief Constable, Miss. It won't take long for him to get here from Derby and Mr. Hanson's in a terrible state. Henry says there's tears running down his cheeks!"

'I do not believe it!' Olinda thought. At the same time she did not say it out loud.

Lucy disappeared and Olinda walked up and down the Sitting-room.

She felt she ought to do something, but she did not know what.

She could not approach the Earl at such a crisis, but it seemed impossible that anyone could suspect, whatever he might have said in the heat of the moment, that he would really kill his own mother.

Once he had worshipped her; once he had loved her so deeply that it had hurt him unbearably when she had fallen short of his ideals and, as he believed, betrayed his father.

But underneath all his bitterness Olinda knew that he did in fact still love her.

That was why it hurt him so much that she should debase herself with a man like Felix Hanson.

'They will soon find out their mistake,' Olinda thought re-assuringly.

But she knew only too well how the words the Earl had uttered would be repeated and perhaps elaborated upon by those who had heard him.

It was an hour later, when she was wondering frantically how she could find out what was happening, that Mrs. Kingston opened the door.

Olinda could see that she had been crying. Her eyes were red and swollen and she said in a low voice which showed she was attempting to keep control of herself:

"The Chief Constable's here, Miss Selwyn, and he asks that all the members of the staff should go into the Hall as he wishes to speak to them. You're not really a member of the staff, but I think perhaps Colonel Gibbon would expect you to be there."

"I would like to come," Olinda replied.

Anything was better than remaining alone in her Sitting-room, isolated from the rest of the household and growing nearly frantic with anxiety.

Mrs. Kingston said no more but preceded Olinda along the passage and through the baize door.

As they descended the Grand Staircase Olinda could see the Chief Constable, wearing his blue uniform with the red sash, standing with his back to the high marble mantelpiece.

The Earl stood beside him and Olinda felt her heart give a sudden leap at the sight of him.

He looked very pale, but he held himself with a dignity that she admired. He did not look up at her as she came down the stairs.

There were a large number of servants already in the Hall. There was also Mr. James Lanceworth, Mr. Thompson, the Curator, and besides the housemaids, Burrows and six of his footmen, including Henry and James.

As soon as Mrs. Kingston and Olinda had reached the bottom of the staircase the Chief Constable said:

"I have come here, as you all know, because your mistress, the Dowager Countess of Kelvedon, has been found dead. She obviously died last night and her lady's-maid informs me that, when she wished to attend to her mistress, as was usual, and help her to bed, she refused her entrance to the room, saying she wished to be alone."

The Chief Constable looked round at the silent audience and said:

"I have however heard a story that Her Ladyship was threatened before dinner when she went upstairs. Where is the Butler?"

"I am here, Sir," Burrows said stepping forward.

"Your name?"

"George Burrows, Sir."

"Tell me, Burrows, what happened when you came into the Hall to announce dinner."

Burrows glanced at the Earl and there was an unhappy expression on his face.

"I want the truth," the Chief Constable said seeing his hesitation. "I have already been told what happened. I wish you to repeat it."

"I heard Her Ladyship and His Lordship quarrelling, Sir, and Her Ladyship said she intended to close the house and dismiss the staff."

The old man paused.

"Go on," the Chief Constable prompted.

"Her Ladyship then told His Lordship that if he wished to keep the place going he could sell the pictures, one by one."

"What did His Lordship say?"

"He said, Sir:—'I'll see you dead first!' "

"Did anyone else hear those exact words?" the Chief Constable enquired.

There was a murmur from James.

"Your name?"

"James Hater, Sir."

"Is what Mr. Burrows has just said the truth?"

"Yes, Sir."

"Who else was present in the Hall?"

"I was, Sir."

"And your name?"

"Henry Jackson, Sir."

"And you heard the same words from His Lordship?"

"Yes, Sir."

Felix Hanson, who was standing in the background, gave an audible sound and put his hands up to his eyes.

The Chief Constable glanced at him, but the Earl did not turn his head.

Then the Chief Constable said:

"Do you admit, My Lord, to saying those particular words, as described by those who heard them?"

"I do," the Earl replied.

There was a silence. One of the housemaids gave a little sob.

"I am of course entitled to reserve my defence until my lawyer is present," the Earl went on, "but I wish to say firmly and categorically that I spoke in the heat of the moment and that I did not murder my mother. If she died by an assailant's hand, it was not mine!"

Now he looked at Felix Hanson who still had his hand over his eyes.

"In the circumstances, My Lord," the Chief Constable said, "you will understand if I ask you to come with me so that the police can take a statement from you."

"Of course," the Earl replied.

It was then that Olinda moved forward.

"May I say something?"

All eyes in the Hall were immediately turned towards her.

She came from behind the servants to face the Chief Constable.

"May I ask your name?" he enquired.

"I am the Honourable Olinda Selwyn, daughter of the late Lord Selwyn, one time Lord Chief Justice of England!"

There was an audible gasp of surprise and the Chief Constable said courteously:

"I remember your father, Miss Selwyn. Will you please proceed?"

"The Earl left the house last night immediately after

141

the remark he made to his mother in this Hall, and went to the island on the lake," Olinda said. "I joined him there soon after nine o'clock."

"How long did you stay with him?" the Chief Constable asked.

"It must have been until nearly two o'clock."

"And did he come back to the house with you?"

"No," Olinda replied. "The Earl said that he would remain on the island for some time; then he would go for a walk, perhaps through the woods and up to the statue which stands on the incline high above the house."

"So you came back alone, Miss Selwyn?"

"I walked back the way I had come," Olinda replied, "through the gardens until I reached the lawns."

She paused before she said:

"I stood for a moment looking at the moonlight shining on the house. Then I saw a man climbing out of a window of Her Ladyship's room!"

There was a silence which seemed to hold everyone in the Hall spellbound.

"As I watched him," Olinda went on, "he clambered down the drain-pipe at the corner of the house."

"Surely that was a rather difficult thing to do?" the Chief Constable asked.

"Not for a man who is very athletic."

"You watched him until he reached the ground?"

"Yes. Then he crossed the lawn and I saw that he carried something wrapped in what appeared to be a white handkerchief. He buried it at the back of one of the flower-beds."

"What did he use to do so?" the Chief Constable enquired.

"His hands," Olinda answered. "Then he crossed the lawn again, opened the catch on one of the Library windows with a pen-knife and stepped inside the house."

There was a moment's complete silence. Then Heyman, the Dowager Countess's maid, gave a shrill cry.

"It was Her Ladyship's jewels he'd taken—the scoundrel! I saw they were missing but was too upset to mention it. I thought perhaps Her Ladyship had put them away somewhere, but they have been stolen—stolen, I tell you!"

"I think you will find them intact at the back of the flower-bed," Olinda said quietly.

"Did you recognise the man you saw climbing down the drain-pipe and burying what I suspect were the jewels?" the Chief Constable enquired.

"Yes," Olinda answered.

"Will you tell me who it was?"

Olinda looked towards Felix Hanson.

For a moment her eyes met his. Then he exclaimed:

"Damn you! All right, I took the jewels! I thought no-one would miss them. But I didn't kill her. She was dead when I found her! Dead, I tell you!"

As his voice rang out hysterically, a servant put a telegram into Olinda's hand.

CHAPTER SEVEN

Olinda walked through the garden and down to the stream which bordered it.

The lawn required cutting and the garden was overgrown except just near the house.

Old Hodges was good with vegetables, but he had 'never been one', as he put it, 'for 'em flowers'.

Nevertheless the great bushes of honeysuckle and wild roses smelt as sweetly as the few cultivated roses which were blooming in a bed her mother had always tended before she became too ill.

Olinda had laid all the flowers which were in bloom on her coffin and they had brought a patch of vivid colour to the sombre greyness of the village Church.

Now, when she had reached the stream, she sat down on a fallen tree-trunk and stared at the water.

But what she saw was the silver surface of the lake at Kelvedon and the grace of the swans as they moved across it.

Always, however hard she tried, her thoughts returned to Kelvedon and the Earl.

Even to think of him was to feel a physical pain between her breasts which she was sure would be with her all her life.

"It is over! It is finished!" she told herself severely. "Why can you not face the truth?"

But she knew she could never escape from the memory of what had happened and the wonder that he had evoked when he had kissed her.

She went to sleep thinking of it. She awoke and the rapture of it was still with her. All the day it accompanied her wherever she went, a ghost that haunted her and could never be exorcised.

She had not seen the Earl before she left Kelvedon.

144

In the dramatic excitement which had followed Felix Hanson's confession, Olinda had opened the telegram which the servant had given her.

When she read what it contained she knew that she must return home immediately.

The telegram had been worded very concisely.

"Please come at once—Nanny."

She knew that the message would never have been sent unless her mother was very ill.

Even so, after a tiring journey that entailed waiting for over two hours for a train from London to Huntingdon, she had not expected that she would arrive to find her mother was dead.

She had known as soon as she saw Nanny's face what had occurred, and she had stood stricken just inside the front door, her hands going out instinctively towards the old woman.

"Her Ladyship died in her sleep," Nanny said. "It was a peaceful end. She went as she would have wished to go."

"Oh, Nanny, why was I not here?" Olinda cried.

"There was nothing you could have done, and none of us expected it," Nanny answered. "The doctor came at the beginning of the week and said Her Ladyship seemed a little better. But he told me yesterday that if she had lived she would have suffered great pain. You would not have wanted that, Miss Olinda."

"No, of course not," Olinda agreed.

"You knew she had cancer?" Nanny asked.

"I suspected it."

"Therefore it was best that she should die as she did," Nanny insisted. "You have to be brave. It's what she'd have expected of you."

As Olinda stood by her mother's bed-side she knew Nanny was right.

It was best that her mother should have died before she suffered the agonising pains which the growth inside her would certainly have caused.

At the same time it was difficult to be brave when someone whom she loved as deeply as she loved her mother had gone from her forever.

'First my father,' she thought, 'then Gerald, and now Mama. I am the only one left!'

There were few relatives to notify of her mother's death, and those there were lived too far away to come to the funeral.

There were two cousins in Cornwall, another in Yorkshire, and a few old cronies who had known her father and who kept in touch with Lady Selwyn at Christmastime.

Otherwise there was no-one to whom she need write or who would be in the least interested in the passing of a woman they had not seen for years.

It was after the funeral was over that Olinda realised she had to decide her own future.

Her mother's pension was halved on her death, which meant, Olinda knew, that as it was mortgaged it would take four years instead of two to pay off Gerald's debt.

There would be just enough, she calculated, for her and Nanny to live at the Manor very frugally, provided she could augment the income by earning a little more.

To think of embroidery brought Kelvedon once again vividly to her mind, and with it the Earl.

'He will have no further need of me,' she had thought when she opened *The Times* two days after she returned home and read:

"We regret to announce the death of the Dowager Countess of Kelvedon suddenly at Kelvedon House, Derbyshire, from a heart attack. The Dowager Countess was forty-seven years of age and was before her marriage to the 9th Earl of Kelvedon, Lady Roseline Alward, daughter of the 2nd Duke of Hull. She married the late Earl in 1857, and there is one son of the mar-

146

*riage who succeeded his father as 10th Earl of Kelve-
don, in 1893."*

"A heart attack!" Olinda said to herself.

That exonerated everyone, even Felix Hanson.

She had, as it happened, believed him when he said
he had found the Dowager Countess dead.

He was a philanderer, selfish, unscrupulous and out for
what he could get, but he was not the stuff of which
murderers are made.

Now, she thought with satisfaction, there would be
no scandal, no crime for anyone to answer, no case to be
brought before the Justices, and the Earl would have
everything he wanted.

"Everything?" a voice asked her mockingly.

"Everything!" she told herself.

She tried to be practical and to use her brain
intelligently.

The Earl had turned to her in his desperation because
she was a stranger. She had come to his rescue at a
moment of complete and utter despair.

She had helped and sustained him, but now her services
were no longer needed. He had come into his Kingdom
and he could easily dispense with the insubstantial woman
to whom he had talked in the darkness.

It was strange, Olinda thought looking back, how they
had always met in the twilight or in the dark.

First of all in the shadows of the Duchesse's bed-room,
then on the island when it had been almost too dark to
see each other's faces. Then under the Goddess of Wisdom
when the sun was sinking, and again on the island in the
moonlight.

"To him I am just a dream," Olinda told herself, "and
just as easily forgotten."

She forced herself to talk to Nanny about their future,
to try to plan ahead.

Yet she knew she was listening with one part of her
mind for a knock on the door, waiting for a telegram, for

a letter, any communication which would tell her that the Earl was still thinking of her!

Perhaps he would be grateful because she had saved him at least for a few hours from the suspicions of the household and of the Chief Constable.

'They would have discovered the truth without my interference,' Olinda thought, 'but perhaps he was glad that he did not have to make a formal statement to the police.'

It was only when she was alone in her own room in the darkness of the night that she could no longer think sensibly of what had happened but must cry miserably because she loved him.

"I love you! I love you!" she would whisper into her pillow and knew that the thought of never seeing him again was so agonising that she wished to die.

It was over a week now since she had buried her mother and the Earl had buried his.

There had been no message from Kelvedon and Olinda's last hope had died.

She watched the stream running over gravel which left it so clear that she could see small fish darting amongst the stones.

The sunlight coming through the branches of the trees cast a speckled glimmer on the water.

She remembered how the stars had been reflected in the lake and the golden light had gleamed from the windows of the great house.

The Earl would now be able to give parties at Kelvedon, parties with his own friends, and the State Rooms would be filled with guests who appreciated their beauty.

The horses in the stables would be ridden, the servants would be busy and the whole place would come alive.

And if it was to be a home, as it should be, then the Earl must marry. Olinda felt a pain stab her at the thought of it, and she knew it had already occurred to him.

Had he not said he had never thought of the pictures

as belonging to him personally but to his son and the Kelvedons who would come after him?

'He must have an heir,' Olinda thought, 'and Kelvedon needs not just one child, but a number of them.'

She thought it was being an only child which had made him feel so intensely about his mother.

He had concentrated all his affection on her and had no brothers or sisters who could have helped him through the shock of learning that she was unfaithful to his father.

"I must pray that he will find love . . real love," Olinda told herself, "and that his wife will give him children to grow up at Kelvedon."

Although she wanted the Earl's happiness, it was impossible not to feel agonised when she imagined another woman in his arms.

He would kiss her and he would evoke in her the wonder and rapture she herself had felt when he kissed her.

Because she could not help it, the tears came into Olinda's eyes and ran down her cheeks so that the sunlight on the stream was blurred and she could no longer see the water clearly.

"Can you really be crying, Olinda?" a voice asked.

She started to her feet but because her tears blinded her it was difficult to see who was standing near her and whom she had not heard approach.

Then the light was there, the brilliant light that had enveloped them both when he had kissed her and it illuminated the Earl so that even through her tears he seemed to come to her in a burst of inexpressible glory.

She stood looking at him until, without really realising she had moved, she was in his arms and he was holding her close against him.

She felt as if everything that had frightened her and which had made her unhappy and insecure vanished at the touch of him.

She was safe. He was holding her!

Then his lips were on hers and they were lost to the world.

There was the wonder, the indescribable ecstasy, the glory and the magic she had known before and she was no longer herself but a part of him.

His kiss was more compelling, more wonderful than it had been when he had kissed her outside the garden-door.

Now, because of what she had suffered, it was like moving from the depths of despair onto the top of the mountains which she had said were impossible to climb, and she was touching the horizon she had never thought to reach.

He kissed her until she could no longer think, but could only vibrate to a music which came from the sky and from her heart.

When at last he raised his head the Earl said in a voice that was unsteady:

"My precious! My sweet dream! I have been longing for this moment!"

"I . . thought you would . . never come," Olinda whispered. "I thought you . . would no longer . . want me."

Her words were incoherent because it was difficult to speak.

But she thought as she looked up at him that she had never seen him look so happy.

"Not want you?" he asked incredulously. "How could you imagine such a thing?"

"You have . . everything . . now."

"Everything but you," he replied. "And you are essential to my happiness, as you must know."

"Am . . I?"

The Earl held her closer.

"What has happened to your instinct?" he asked. "That wise little instinct which helped and guided me and made me believe I could do anything, even manage to preserve Kelvedon without any money."

He paused to look down into her eyes. Then he said: "I believe, that with your help, I could have done it."

"Of . . course you . . could!"

"But not without you."

Then he was kissing her again, kissing her with long slow, possessive kisses that seemed to draw not only her heart from her body, but also her mind and her soul and make them his. . . .

Later they sat side by side on the fallen tree-trunk.

"I could not get away before," the Earl explained. "There were so many things to see to, so many relations who came to the funeral and would not leave as quickly as I would have liked."

He paused and knew without Olinda asking the question what she wanted to know.

"My mother had apparently suffered with her heart for some time," he said in a low voice. "The doctor had warned her not to exert herself, and on no account to become emotionally upset."

He paused before he went on:

"He had treated her for many years and knew how dangerous and depleting her anger could be."

"You did not know this?" Olinda enquired.

The Earl shook his head.

"My mother would never speak of her health. She thought it made her seem old and anyway, as you know, I had been away for two years."

There was a note in his voice as if he blamed himself and Olinda said quickly:

"You would have done no good if you had come back sooner and I think it was the way, had she been given the choice, your mother would have wished to die, while she was still beautiful."

"That is true," the Earl agreed, "but if she had died twenty-four hours sooner she would not have suffered from Hanson's perfidy or my stupidity."

Again the pain was in his voice and Olinda's hands tightened on his.

"You are not to blame yourself," she said. "You have to be sensible about this and realise it is all for the best. Your father would not have wished you to be shut out from your inheritance."

"It is no use regretting," the Earl agreed. "You must help me to look forward, Olinda."

"You know I want to do that," she said softly.

"But because I shall always feel partly to blame for my mother's death," the Earl said, "I have been generous where Felix Hanson is concerned."

Olinda looked at him enquiringly and he went on:

"My mother had written him a cheque for £8,000. He admitted that she had intended to cancel it, but I told him he could keep the money."

"I am glad you did that," Olinda said.

"He has also taken away the car my mother gave him."

He smiled spontaneously as he added:

"That was not a very generous act on my part. I dislike cars. I so much prefer my horses."

"So do I," Olinda answered.

"They are waiting for you to ride them."

She gave a little sigh of sheer happiness and turned her face against the Earl's shoulder.

"There are so many things for us to do together, my darling," he said. "But most of all I want to talk to you. I never thought to say that to a woman, but there is so much to discuss, so much perhaps to argue about in the future, that we shall never be bored even if we spend a great deal of our lives at Kelvedon."

"That is what I want to do," Olinda said.

"Do you really mean that or are you saying it to please me?"

He put his hand under her chin and tipped her face up so that he could look into her eyes.

"Do you realise I have never looked at you properly in the day-time?" he asked.

"I was thinking that just now," Olinda said. "We have always met in the darkness."

"A dream from the night," he said softly. "But you are even more beautiful, my precious, when I see you with the sun on your hair and the light of it in your eyes."

He looked at her face as if he was taking in every

detail until her eye-lids fell and a faint flush rose in her cheeks.

"You are .. making me .. shy," she protested.

"I adore you when you are shy," he said. "I think I have been rather afraid of the wise follower of the Goddess Athene who has told me what to do, who has set me impossible tasks and given me ideals which seemed to be completely out of reach."

He spoke softly and yet there was a note in his voice that made Olinda quiver.

"And now," he went on, "I find not an Amazon or a Joan of Arc, but someone very young and very lovely who can blush—something I thought women had forgotten how to do."

Olinda gave a little murmur and moved against his fingers which were holding her chin, but his lips were on hers and once again she was his captive. . . .

When he raised his head he said:

"I have remembered something!"

"What is it?" Olinda asked.

"When I saw you in the shadows by the Duchesse's bed something stirred in my mind. You reminded me of someone, but I could not think who it was."

"Who .. was it?"

"The Virgin in Leonardo da Vinci's first picture of the Annunciation!"

There was a note of reverence in the Earl's voice as he went on:

"It was the picture he painted when he was very young, and the Angel Gabriel comes to Mary at dusk. The bluish-green of the evening makes nature a part of the miracle and the Virgin's hair is pale gold against it."

He kissed Olinda's hair.

"I have looked at that picture so often in the Louvre and it meant something special to me. Now I know it was you!"

Olinda hid her face against his shoulder.

"I am so .. glad, so very, very glad .. you should .. think of me like .. that. I thought .."

"What did you think?"

"That you would consider me . . fast and . . immodest because I let you . . kiss me."

"Could I imagine you were anything but pure and perfect?"

He kissed her eyes and her forehead.

"There is so much for me to discover about you," he said. "So much I want to know, so much that I never thought to find in any woman."

"I am afraid . . you may be . . disappointed," Olinda whispered.

"How could I be?" he enquired. "Did you not tell me that real love involves the heart, the brain and the soul?"

He waited for her reply, then when she would have spoken took the words from her lips with his. . . .

Later when they could speak again, he said:

"I am conceited enough, my precious to believe I can capture your heart."

"It is yours . . already," Olinda whispered.

"And your mind will force me to exert myself, because many of the subjects in which I was interested have been forgotten, and my knowledge has become rusty while I wasted my time in Paris."

"I am sure you are as clever as your father," Olinda said. "I read that he was admired and respected by everybody."

"And if you are as clever as yours," the Earl said, "I tremble to think how erudite our children will be!"

"I want them to be just like you," Olinda said and she blushed again as she spoke.

"I think they will have a great deal of their mother's character," the Earl smiled, "and certainly her beauty. Do you realise how beautiful you are, my darling?"

"Please . . tell me," Olinda begged. "No-one ever has."

"I will tell you until I convince you that you are the most beautiful person I have ever seen," he answered, "but I have not quite finished. There is a third part of the love of which we talked—the soul."

"You do believe we have one?"

"I believe you have," he answered. "I want you to help me find mine."

He drew her a little closer to him as he said:

"When I was thinking of you and longing for the time to pass so that I could come to you, I looked up in a book in the Library all you told me about the Duchesse de Mazarin. You were right, Olinda. She made the King very happy because she gave him what none of his other loves had done."

"She inspired him!"

"And that is what you have done to me! She brought him a new awareness of life, and you have given me that also. And most important of all she gave him the love that he had always sought but failed to find."

"Can . . I give you . . that?"

"You have given it to me already," the Earl said. "You have brought me a love that I did not know even existed— a love so glorious, so perfect—and I know you are right, Olinda, it is part of the Divine."

"That is what I . . thought when you . . first kissed me," Olinda whispered, "but I was . . afraid you did not . . feel as I . . did."

"I knew that first kiss was quite different from any other kiss I had ever given or received," the Earl replied. "But because it was so intense, so wonderful, I was afraid!"

"Afraid?" Olinda asked.

"That it was not real, that I was imagining the ecstasy of it."

He paused before he said:

"I had not intended to kiss you. I had enjoyed talking to you, but somehow until that moment I had thought of you not as a desirable woman, but just as somebody understanding and ethereal, a being from out of this world."

"And when you . . kissed me?" Olinda asked.

"Then I knew you were what I had always been seeking, the woman who was meant for me, and was part of me."

"You did not .. say so."

"I was too bewildered, and for the moment so surprised, so spellbound by the wonder of your lips that I did not know what to do or what to say! After I left you, Olinda, I went to the Temple to think about you."

"If .. only I had .. known," Olinda murmured, remembering how miserable she had been, thinking he would consider her fast and immodest.

"I could hardly believe it had really happened," the Earl said, "and then the next night when you came to me when I was so desperate and I thought I had lost Kelvedon, I did not kiss you because we were so close to each other mentally that I felt our bodies should not intrude upon our minds."

"I understood .. that," Olinda said.

"I thought you would."

Then to Olinda's surprise he stood up and drew her to her feet.

"Now, my darling, there are no inhibitions and no reason for us to deny our love," he said. "We belong to each other in every way, and the only thing I want is that you should become my wife as quickly as possible!"

"You are in .. mourning," Olinda said in a low voice.

"As you are," he answered. "Your Nurse told me what had happened when I arrived. I am so sorry, my dearest, it must have been very upsetting for you."

"I would not have wished my mother to suffer."

"I can understand that, but it leaves us both free, free to be together, Olinda. I cannot wait on convention or on the proper period of mourning."

She looked at him wide-eyed as he said:

"One of the reasons I was a little longer than I meant in coming to you was that I stopped the night in London so that I could obtain a Special Licence. Are you prepared to listen to what I have planned?"

"You know .. I am."

He thought as he looked at her that all the sunshine from the sky was concentrated in her grey eyes.

"We will get married very quietly and secretly because

our marriage cannot be announced for some months, and I will then take you to my house in Leicestershire."

"Not to Kelvedon?"

"Not for our honeymoon," he answered with a smile. "I do not wish you to be jealous of it and I want to concentrate completely and absolutely on my wife until she is sure that I love her more than anything in the world—even more than Kelvedon!"

"Do you . . really mean . . that?" Olinda asked.

"I mean it!" he replied. "And although it may be hard to prove, I intend that you shall believe me!"

He reached out his arms and drew her roughly against him.

"You have to believe me," he said masterfully, "and this is the one thing about which I shall brook no argument. Do you understand?"

Olinda gave a laugh of sheer happiness.

"I want to . . believe you."

He kissed her passionately and she felt a flame rise within her to respond to the fire on his lips and in his eyes.

"You are mine!" he said. "Every precious part of you, and I promise you, my sweet, you will have no rival, only interests that we will share and will belong to us together."

"I love . . you!" Olinda whispered. "I want to . . make you . . happy."

"That is what you have made me already," he answered. "And there is all the future for us to discover how great and marvellous that happiness can be!"

He turned her towards the house and said with a sudden urgency in his voice:

"Why are we wasting time? Let us get married, my precious! I am so afraid that you are, after all, only a dream, and that when night comes you will vanish and I will lose you."

"You will never do that."

"Again you are right," the Earl replied, "for you will be with me during the day and I shall hold you in my arms all night. That should make sure that you cannot escape."

He looked down at her face in the sunshine and as if he could not help himself he once again sought her lips. Then resolutely he took his arms from her and taking her by the hand started walking back towards the house.

They moved towards the garden, but when they reached the bushes of wild roses and honeysuckle the Earl stopped.

"Is this really happening to us?" he asked. "To you and me, Olinda? Is it possible for a man to move from the hell of despondency into such a Heaven of happiness?"

"It is possible when two people are . . in love," Olinda said. "I told you that real love is like the . . Holy Grail and yet it is . . possible to find it."

"As we have!" the Earl said.

She looked at him with a radiance in her face that he had never seen on any other woman's.

"As we have, my sweet dream," he repeated very gently.

His lips found hers and they were no longer in a garden in the sunshine but had reached the top of an inaccessible mountain and were enveloped in the brilliant, blinding light of the Divine.

THE END

FROM HELL TO HEAVEN BY BARBARA CARTLAND

The Derby of 1831 finishes in a dead heat due to the jockey riding the horse of the Earl of Branscombe, bumping and obstructing the horse belonging to the Marquis of Alchester. The Marquis is furious and his anger increases when he learns that the Earl has confided in the Princess Lieven that he intends to marry his Ward, who is a great heiress.

Wondering what he can do to circumvent the Earl's plans, the Marquis goes to the country with his close friend Peregrine Wallingham, and finds in one of the Orphanages on his Estate that the children are starving, owing to the crookedness of the Matron and his Agent.

There is one orphan, the daughter of two missionaries who died of cholera in India, who is older than the rest and on meeting Kistna the Marquis has a brilliant idea of how he can pay the Earl back in his own coin.

How Kistna is taken from a Hell of starvation, privation and misery to the Heaven of the Marquis's magnificent ancestral house and how after many twists and turns of fate the Earl gets his just deserts, is told in this exciting and dramatic 276th book by Barbara Cartland.

ISBN 0 552 11600 9   95p

BARBARA CARTLAND'S
LIBRARY OF LOVE

WHILE EVERY EFFORT IS MADE TO KEEP PRICES LOW, IT IS
SOMETIMES NECESSARY TO INCREASE PRICES AT SHORT NOTICE.
CORGI BOOKS RESERVE THE RIGHT TO SHOW AND CHARGE NEW
RETAIL PRICES ON COVERS WHICH MAY DIFFER FROM THOSE
ADVERTISED IN THE TEXT OR ELSEWHERE.

THE PRICES SHOWN BELOW WERE CORRECT AT THE TIME OF GOING
TO PRESS (DECEMBER '81)

☐ 10543 0	THE HUNDRETH CHANCE No. 5	*Ethel M. Dell*	60p
☐ 10560 0	THE REASON WHY No. 6	*Elinor Glyn*	60p
☐ 10588 0	THE WAY OF AN EAGLE No. 7	*Ethel M. Dell*	60p
☐ 10624 0	THE VICISSITUDES OF EVANGELINE No. 8	*Elinor Glyn*	65p
☐ 10644 5	THE BARS OF IRON No. 9	*Ethel M. Dell*	65p
☐ 10670 4	MAN AND MAID No. 10	*Elinor Glyn*	65p
☐ 10704 2	THE SONS OF THE SHEIK No. 11	*E. M. Hull*	65p
☐ 10758 1	SIX DAYS No. 12	*Elinor Glyn*	65p
☐ 10760 3	RAINBOW IN THE SPRAY No. 13	*Pamela Wynne*	65p
☐ 10843 X	THE GREAT MOMENT No. 14	*Elinor Glyn*	70p
☐ 10844 8	GREATHEART No. 15	*Ethel M. Dell*	70p
☐ 10929 0	THE BROAD HIGHWAY No. 16	*Jeffery Farnol*	70p
☐ 10930 4	THE SEQUENCE No. 17	*Elinor Glyn*	70p
☐ 12140 5	THE LION TAMER No. 24	*E. M. Hull*	70p
☐ 12190 1	IT No. 24	*Elinor Glyn*	70p
☐ 12392 0	FRECKLES No. 26	*Gene Stratton Porter*	70p
☐ 12346 7	LEAVE IT TO LOVE No. 27	*Pamela Wynne*	75p
☐ 12615 6	RAMAZAN THE RAJAH	*Vere Lockwood*	75p
☐ 12616 4	THE MONEY MOON	*Jeffery Farnol*	75p

Titles by Barbara Cartland and Published by Corgi Books

☐ 11705 6	**THE LIONESS AND THE LILY**	*Barbara Cartland*	95p
☐ 11600 9	**FROM HELL TO HEAVEN**	*Barbara Cartland*	95p
☐ 11787 0	**DOLLARS FOR THE DUKE**	*Barbara Cartland*	95p

*All these books are available at your bookshop or newsagent, or can be ordered direct
from the publisher. Just tick the titles you want and fill in the form below.*

CORGI BOOKS, Cash Sales Department, P.O. Box 11, Falmouth, Cornwall.

Please send cheque or postal order, no currency.

Please allow cost of book(s) plus the following for postage and packing:

U.K. CUSTOMERS. 40p for the first book, 18p for the second book and 13p for each
additional book ordered, to a maximum charge of £1.49.

B.F.P.O. & EIRE. Please allow 40p for the first book, 18p for the second book plus 13p
per copy for the next three books, thereafter 7p per book.

OVERSEAS CUSTOMERS. Please allow 60p for the first book plus 18p per copy for
each additional book.

NAME (Block letters) ....

ADDRESS ....

....